·A GYPSY BROTHERS EPILOGUE·

LILI ST. GERMAIN

This paperback also contains bonus novella *Alternate*

Zero Hour

ISBN-13: 978-1545197127
ISBN-10: 1545197121

Cover Designer: Hang Le
Formatting: Champagne Formats

Other Books by Lili St. Germain

THE GYPSY BROTHERS SERIES

Seven Sons

Six Brothers

Five Miles

Four Score

Three Years

Two Roads

One Love

Zero Hour

Alternate (short novella)

THE CARTEL TRILOGY

Cartel

Kingpin

Empire

THE CALIFORNIA BLOOD SERIES

Verona Blood

Burn in Your Blood

In Cold Blood

THE SKULLS CARTEL SERIES

The Prospect

Queenpin

THE VAMPIRELAND SERIES

Walking Dead Girl

The Vessel

STANDALONE NOVELS

Gun Shy (Psychological Thriller)

Afterward (Contemporary Romance)

BEFORE YOU BEGIN!

You're reading this book because you've read the Gypsy Brothers series books 1-7. Did you know Lili also released a novella called ALTERNATE which has chapters from Dornan, Jase and Elliot's point of view?

It's highly recommended (but not essential) that you read ALTERNATE before this book. Flip to page 131 to check it out!

It will have blood; they say, blood will have blood.

—MacBeth, *SHAKESPEARE*

CHAPTER ONE

Juliette

There's a storm coming.

I know this even before I open my eyes and gulp at the air, my gaze glued to the ceiling as I try to catch my breath. I know this even as I turn my head to the right and press shaking fingers against his stubbled cheek, as I look into the eyes of the son and realize they're not his father's.

"Hey," Jase whispers gently, his voice devoid of that throaty rasp he gets when he's been asleep. His dark brown eyes are bloodshot, and I can tell he's barely rested. I feel selfish, because I managed to get a couple of hours, and he's gotten none. Again.

I soften as he presses those full, lush lips to my fingers. "Good morning."

I am safe. Dornan is dead. Jase is with me. It's my mantra, words that I repeat over and over.

I am safe.

Dornan is dead.

Jase is with me.

The second and third are true, but the first is a lie. We're no safer than we were the day we were born into the Gypsy Brothers Motorcycle Club, pawns in a war we knew nothing about yet were created because of. There's Jase, conceived in some illicit tryst, born in secret, hundreds of miles away from our fathers. His mother was smart; she likely hightailed it out of L.A. the day she peed on the stick and it gave her two lines. And then me, daughter of the President of the Gypsy Brothers, born and cradled in the very arms of evil himself. Dornan Ross. He wasn't my daddy, but he was the first person who ever held me, the first person who ever touched me apart from the doctor who caught me as my mother farewelled me into the world and then pretty much abandoned me.

Our beginnings couldn't have been more different, but our blood meant we ended up in exactly the same place: here.

But my bones don't lie, and they tell me there's a storm brewing outside. I squeeze Jase's hand once, certain I won't be getting any more sleep today.

He pulls his hand away and turns away from me, moving into a sitting position on his side of the bed. "I'm taking a shower," he says, getting up and going into the bathroom.

I watch, silently, as he closes the door.

The lock clicks over on the other side and I flinch.

He's locking me out.

He's never done that before.

It's probably nothing personal, I try to assuage myself. Everyone needs their time alone.

I hear the water come on, the glass shower door clink shut, and

ZERO HOUR

I watch the door.
It feels personal.
He's locking me out.
He's pushing me away.
I can't say I blame him.
Honestly, after all the shit that's gone down?
I'm surprised he's still here at all.

CHAPTER TWO

Jase

Jase …. The baby … It's yours.

I don't sleep anymore. Was never great at sleeping anyway, but now, sleep is something I rarely do.

It's too late to stop the contractions.

Juliette fights sleep just as much as me, but she's been through more than I have. Her body—and her mind—are closer to breaking point than mine. She's still recovering from the torture and the mental abuse my father rained down on her in the three months she vanished, the three months when I fought to find her.

I still can't believe I was such an ass. After the way we fought, I assumed she'd left, and my father's cryptic excuse that she'd left town should have alerted me. But I was hurting. She broke my fucking heart, showed up like a ghost, made me fall in love with her all over again, and then she walked out and went back to him. And she had my baby inside her when she did it. Neither of us knew, and that's the worst part of all. If she'd stayed. If I'd found her sooner. Maybe our daughter would be here with us.

I know why she went back to Dornan after he woke up from his coma. I'd been on my own quest for vengeance for three blood-fueled years, since my father let me out of the cage he'd locked me in the day Juliette died. The day I was forced to watch as my father and my brothers almost killed her. And the birth. It's been eight months since we lost the baby, six since she shot and killed Dornan. We had a brief respite in Colorado after shit went down in Furnace Creek, but it wasn't long before the Cartel closed ranks and came baying for our blood. We ran to New York, then Virginia, and now we're holed up in a shitty walk-up in Miami, not because we don't have money but because we're trying to blend in. They keep finding us in the expensive boltholes, so we thought we'd change tacks and sandwich ourselves in the seediest part of town, amongst the pimps and the drug dealers. I shaved my hair off, military-short, and let my clean-shaven face morph into a three-day stubble; Juliette's hair is still long, because I refused to let her cut it short just to try and evade them, but it's bright red now. She jokes that it makes her look like a hooker, but her smile fades too quickly when she says it, and I know she's completely fucking confused about who she is and how she fits into this world.

We're a sorry-looking pair. I won't sleep, she won't eat, and between the two of us, we fit in to Biscayne Boulevard's worst apartment block just fine.

It's my fault our baby died, Julz said, after we left the hospital empty-handed.

It is. It's not. You didn't know any better. *Why didn't you just tell me what he'd done to you?*

All the things I didn't say.

There's only so long a person can operate on autopilot, pulling together the pieces of charred wreckage and escaping one last time before the big one hits. There are only so many places you can hide before you just plain run out of dark corners to cower in.

I'm not a coward. I don't hide. But here, now?

I don't know what else to do to keep her safe.

She's right here beside me, but I can feel her slipping away. I'm losing her. I'm losing us. I don't know what to do. It's like being trapped in a three-by-three cell all over again. It's like being held under water and deciding when to take that first gasp of water that's going to make you drown. It's like holding hands, both your palms slicked with your collective blood, in a fucking nightmare that never ends.

Sometimes, when I'm really tired, I see things. I see *him*. In the corner of my eye, Dornan Ross looms, even though he's dead and buried. I don't tell Julz what I see, because she'll probably start to see him as well.

Shit, she probably already does.

Sometimes, I can't tell if I'm starting to become him. My father. *Dornan*. The way I am, the things I've done—they make Juliette's sins look like child's play.

Of course, I'd never tell her that. I'll never tell her the things I've done.

It doesn't mean she won't find out anyway.

A girl. It's a girl. Barely as long as an envelope in my open palms.

My daughter. I still remember the way my tears fell onto her tiny little face as she lived and died all in one breath.

I miss her.

CHAPTER THREE

Juliette

As soon as Jase is out of the bathroom, his bare chest still covered in glistening beads of water, I pounce on him.

Yeah. I'm that desperate.

He attempts a small smile as he tries to push past me, to the small duffel bag that holds his clothes.

I don't let him. I lean down and suck his nipple into my mouth, smiling as his cock reacts when my teeth brush against his sensitive skin.

"Julz," he breathes, his cock swelling against my belly. The way he says my name doesn't make me melt, though. It makes me swallow away tears and kiss him harder so he won't talk anymore. The way he says my name, it's like he doesn't want to be here with me at all. I hear his internal struggle. I see his frustration. I feel the rage that rolls off him in waves, the rage I thought I'd only ever see in Dornan. I was wrong. It's in the boy I love, too, like a poison in his bloodstream. He's so angry. He's so angry at me for the things I've done, and he thinks I can't see it, but I can. Even when he makes love to me, he's angry.

Before I can reach up to kiss him again, Jase takes my wrists and spins me around, kicking at my ankles to open my legs wider. I'm already soaked just at the thought of him inside me, and my breath hitches in my throat as his fingers pull my panties to the side and slide along my wet pussy.

He pushes me down so my face is against the mattress, my ass in the air and slams his cock into me in one excruciating motion that hurts and burns and almost makes me come. We have sex right there, me bent over the side of the bed and Jase fucking me from behind, hard and fast and carnal, and it's the only fifteen minutes of the day that I feel anything except broken and afraid.

I'm such a fucking stereotype. After he pulls out and comes over my back and my ass, he leaves me alone on the bed, naked and marked. I wait until he leaves the room, and then I bury my face in the comforter and cry.

CHAPTER FOUR

Jase

It makes me sick to my stomach that I don't want to touch Julz. It's almost torturous having to fuck her, because I simultaneously want to push her away and fuck her until she's crying. I can't reconcile the way I want to consume her and reject her all at once. Well, I can, actually.

I still haven't told her about what happened after she 'died', after Elliot whisked her away from the hospital in Los Angeles and hid her in Nebraska six-and-change years ago. Still haven't told her the things my father made me do, the perverted things I'd come to enjoy. She thinks I'm good inside.

She's deluded.

The girl's smart, though. She knows there's something dark

inside me that wants to come out. She keeps asking me to tell her, with that soft throaty whisper and those endless green eyes tilted up at me. She wants to know all the secrets that fester inside me, but if I ever, ever told her, she'd know that I was worse than my father ever was.

They say the apple never falls far from the tree, and I'd say this apple never fucking fell, *period.* I'm the shiny apple that might've looked the best on the surface—different to the rest of them, full of promise that there was another way—but they broke me. They made me worse than any of them could ever be.

I hurt people. I hurt women.

I killed people.

And that's not even the worst of it.

The first man I ever killed was John Portland, and I cried as I pulled the trigger. Yeah, I was a stupid kid and he begged me to do it, and yeah, it was a mercy killing, but it doesn't matter. Point is, his life was the first one I took—*I killed Juliette's father, for Christ's sake*—and after I ended his life with a single bullet, delivered in the dark in a dirty basement, I didn't stop.

I couldn't stop.

The second person I ever killed wasn't a mercy killing. It was a cop. I killed a cop because my father handed me a gun and said it was me or him, and I chose him. I always chose them.

I was a fucking coward. A lovesick, blood-fueled fucking coward.

The last person I killed was Donny, my last surviving brother, and that was eight months ago. I ripped his fucking eyeball out before I butchered him, and the one single thing that stopped me from dismembering him was knowing that Juliette was watching me. Her screams broke through my haze of red, as I took Donny's own knife and sunk it into his flesh, again and again, so deep it hit bone more than once. I severed the tendons that made his arms work, so he was putty underneath me. I straddled my own brother and thrust upon him the vengeful punishment that they all deserved. For Julz. For my mother. For *everything*.

I killed him, and I haven't killed since.

I'm hungry. My palms are itching. It's *torture*.

I don't know how long I'm going to last before I have to draw blood again.

CHAPTER FIVE

Juliette

I feel like I'm losing Jase.

He goes away and leaves me here with Elliot, and I don't know where he's going. Since the Cartel found us in Colorado, they found Elliot and his family, too. We've all been moving and running, keeping our heads low and our guns drawn until we can figure this shit out. The DEA makes all sorts of promises about arresting Julian, Emilio's brother and the new kingpin of this whole operation, but they keep stalling. They need more evidence. They need a stronger case. In the meantime, Elliot's dragging his ex-girlfriend and his little girl around the country, holing up in a different place every week or two. His little daughter is so freaked out, she'll barely speak. Elliot's a wreck, and Amy seems to be the only one holding it together. She's a psychologist, so maybe she's got some kind of technique to avoiding freaking the fuck out that the rest of us lack.

We're all just sitting ducks, or at least that's what it feels like. If we do anything, the DEA notices.

The DEA is keeping us waiting, feeding us empty promises while they continue to remind us what we owe them. Testimony in court. They say Jase and I will get immunity for the things we've done, so long as we testify against the Cartel and the Gypsy Brothers, but is it really that simple? Will it really be a case of us just telling our stories and then being given a free pass? The way Tommy tells it, the people in charge of the case are pissed that I started killing them all off. They're pissed that Dornan's sons and his father Emilio are dead, and they're even more pissed that Tommy turned a blind eye back in Furnace Creek and gave me the time I needed to shoot Dornan dead once and for all. Tommy's been kicked off the case and reassigned to an undercover gig somewhere on the west coast, Elliot's being blackmailed to work for the DEA, and Jase and I have the strangest feeling that we're being set up by the very people who claim to want to help us. It's the one thing we can talk about without averted eyes and misunderstandings. Figuring out what the DEA want with us, and how we're all going to get out of this alive and intact. We can't talk about Dornan … can't talk about the baby we lost … but we can talk about the fucking Drug Enforcement Agency until our faces go numb.

The DEA says they need more evidence before they can arrest Emilio's brother, Julian Ross, and bring him to trial. But I'm not so sure that's what they need.

What they need is a drum of gasoline and a match. What they need is to trap every goddamned Gypsy Brother and Il Sangue Cartel member inside the clubhouse and set fire to the fucking place. How else will any of us ever be safe? We might be standing now, but it's only a matter of time before they find us and kill us, piece by piece. It's the thing that keeps me awake at night: not if, but when. When are they going to find us?

What are they going to do to us when they do?

I might have survived what Dornan did to me, but I was different then. Younger. Stupider. I've had too much time to think since I got out of the cage he locked me in. I've lost our daughter. I've caused so many people to be living in real fear of being cut down at any moment.

I'm the reason Elliot's grandmother was murdered. Dornan might've used his hands to beat her to death, but it was because of me and the things I did to his sons and his club.

Mostly, though, I've had too much time to sit and think about my vengeance. How it's a false victory, because it never ends, not really. There's always going to be somebody else who wants their pound of flesh. I could have stayed dead, stayed in Nebraska and cheered the fuck up and maybe convinced Elliot to stay with me. I could have been a normal person. And instead I've created a war that spans countries and families for generations, a war paid for in lives and blood. Terrifyingly, a war where every side believes they're doing the right thing, because nobody can remember anymore where it all began. Who threw the first stone. Who fired the first bullet.

Who stole the first heart they weren't supposed to steal.

Yeah, I think about revenge a lot. When I'm thinking of the way the light dimmed in Dornan's dying eyes and the way he said *you killed my sons.* How beautiful it was, and how hollow.

CHAPTER SIX

Jase

My father murdered my mother when I was sixteen years old, and I was the lucky SOB who got to find her. He shot her first, not somewhere where she'd bleed to death right away, but somewhere where it'd hurt. After he shot her, he told me later, he beat her, while she begged him to stop.

The gunshot? The beating? She would have survived them both. He didn't want to kill her with his violence. He just wanted to make her think she might survive his fury. Even as he was killing her, he was cruel enough to make her think she had a hope of making it out alive.

I often wonder if she knew that he was there to kill her. Maybe she'd clung to some hope that he'd just beat her to a bloody pulp as retribution for running away from him with his unborn son. With me.

Before I'd been born, I was already the reason my mother was doomed to die.

Sixteen fucking years and change, she evaded him. Found a group of people she could trust. Lived simply. Sent me to the local public school with a name that couldn't be traced back to my father in any way. I didn't even know he'd existed, not at first, not until I'd started snooping around and demanding to know who my dad was. All the other kids had dads. Even if their dads were losers or dead or cheating on their moms—they knew where they'd come from. I wanted to know why my mom had blonde hair and skin as pale as snow, and why I had these black eyes and olive skin and dark hair that didn't match one piece of her.

I threatened my mom. I was going to find out, one way or another, who my father was.

So she told me, eventually. And as soon as she did—as soon as she said, Dornan Ross is your father, I wished she'd kept me in the dark. Lied to me. *Your father kills people*, she'd said. *He's a very, very bad man. You're nothing like him.*

My poor dead mother and the way she believed she'd saved me from this family. *You're nothing like him.*

I'm everything like him.

Sometimes I imagine what life would have been like if she'd lived. If they'd never found us, living peacefully, in our simple house in Colorado. Shopping at thrift stores because we had no money, eating fucking beans and the bread they marked down the day after it started to go stale, trudging to school in the snow in winter with my beaten-up sneakers that didn't quite keep the cold, melted ice from seeping in. It was blissful fucking ignorance, and in an instant it was all taken away.

My father murdered my mother. He shot her and beat her and

finally, when he'd broken half the bones in her body, he dumped her in a bathtub and shot her up with enough heroin to kill five men.

I like to think her death was quick. That she didn't suffer. But I've watched my father kill plenty of people between then and now, and I think, the way he loved her, the way she left him when she found out she was pregnant with me? I think her death was anything but quick.

That's how I found her. Motionless, covered in blood, the syringe still hanging out of her pale arm. I'd been late home, that day. I don't think it would have mattered, if I could have saved her, because even though I was late home, she was stone cold by the time I'd dragged her up out of the tub and tried to shake her back to life in my arms.

"Mom," I'd whispered. "*Mom*?"

I shook her. I shook her so fucking hard.

She didn't wake up.

"MOM!" I screamed.

My father confronted me. I knew he was my father the moment our eyes locked; they were the same eyes I looked at when I saw myself in the mirror every morning. My eyes were his eyes, and I was so fucking angry that this was the way he'd chosen for us to meet. I'd always held this weird kind of hope that he was a good man, better than my mother had told me, but he was so much worse than she ever let on.

"You know who I am?" he asked me.

I opened my mouth. Closed it again. Looked down at my mother, who I was still holding onto. I remember how slippery she was, how she had so much blood on her that it'd never all dry. Most of all, I remember the rage that consumed me when I saw what he'd done to her.

I launched at him. Even then, as I punched and kicked and

rained down blows on him, an unsettling realization was creeping into my gut. He wasn't just my father. He was the thing in my nightmares, the promise of what I'd one day become. The darkness I'd been trying to resist my whole life, when I looked at the hollow of a girl's neck and marveled how my palm would cut off her breath *just like that*. The thing inside me that enjoyed the sight of blood, the thing that drove me to fight and drink and hurt people. My mother might have been my solace in the first sector of my life, some kind of earth angel who called me back from the reality of the Ross blood surging through my veins, but when I stared into my father's eyes for the first time, all I saw was my worst self.

He'd overpowered me so easily. One well placed blow to my head and I was out, my last sensation the way my skull whacked against the sunflower-printed tile. A sharp prick at my arm and I was out, floating on blackness, a warm fog that felt oddly comforting. I could still hear bits and pieces of conversation. I remember a woman's low voice, a warm palm on my forehead. I remember rolling around in the trunk of a car, unable to move. I remember wetting myself, hog-tied and unconscious, the warm piss turning cold almost instantly.

I remember Juliette, the first kind face in a sea of people who said they were my family, but who treated me like I was the enemy.

I remember being held down by my brothers, people I didn't even know, as *Gypsy Brothers* was tattooed all the way across my back, a brand to make sure I could never be anything but his son from that moment on. As my father watched proudly, my mother's blood still under his fingernails, I yelled until I was hoarse.

I remember the way *she* crept into the room I was interred in afterwards, my beautiful Juliette. My eyes fell on her and I knew she was something else. Something I didn't want to hurt. Something I wanted to keep safe.

Ironic, then, that it was *she* who kept *me* safe. Wiped away the blood on my back, scrubbed my mother's dried blood from my palms, brought me clothes and a soft blanket to wrap around myself.

I remember my father had eventually tried to apologize to me, in some bizarre way. The word *sorry* never passed his lips, but I could tell even he was kind of shocked at what he'd done. I listened to his rumination about my mother, about how she'd stolen me away, and a film of ice began to form over my heart.

I looked at the man who'd helped create me, and I saw a monster.

When he was done trying to justify his actions, he fell silent. Waiting for me to respond.

"How the hell did she ever look at you?" I asked him, eventually. "That's the part I don't understand. How the hell did a woman like my mother ever get involved with somebody like you?"

My dad set his jaw, ran his hand through his hair.

"Who said I gave her a choice?" he replied, and I'm pretty sure that was the most honest thing he ever said to me in my entire life.

I settled into my psychotic family, a sleeper agent of sorts—somebody who knew he was powerless to take immediate action, but who understood that vengeance is a long game, not a short one. I assimilated—eventually—and my father thought I'd accepted my fate of being his son.

I accepted nothing. I learned to ride the motorcycle they bestowed upon me. I wore the leather cut, bore the tattoos they insisted on marking me with, and I did as I was told, all the while waiting for the moment when I'd be able to turn on them all and destroy my demented family from within. A ticking time bomb, I was, and it was the thought of avenging my mother's senseless murder that fueled my existence.

I didn't mean to fall in love with Julz. I was only a kid, and she was even younger than me, but from that very first night when she crept into my room, green eyes open wide with pity and shock, she was mine. I fell hard, I fell instantly, and I vowed that her fate wouldn't match my mother's because I would protect her.

And yet, less than a year later, I was watching—and screaming—as my brother Chad smacked his hand over her mouth and raped her. He was the first, but he wasn't the last—my father saved that for himself. Tied her to a chair, naked and bleeding, and interrogated her, for betraying the club, along with her father.

The night before it happened, before my Juliette was murdered, I'd climbed a mess of tangled vines to sneak through her bedroom window. Her father was already planning his betrayal of the club, and we had front row tickets to get the fuck out of LA and away from the Gypsy Brothers.

We'd been inexperienced, fumbling teenagers—she more so than me—and we'd almost had sex that night, but I'd stopped. *I want it to be special for you*, I'd said to her. I didn't want to take her virginity in secret in her bedroom. I wanted it to be special. I wanted her to feel loved. I could wait, I told her. I'd wait forever for her.

And then, the next day, I watched as my brothers took that from her, the very thing I'd been trying to protect. As they raped her and beat her and laughed as she cried.

She hadn't done anything wrong, except be born to a father who would try and betray mine.

She hadn't done anything wrong, but they still destroyed her, hour by hour, brother by brother, until all that was left was a naked, bloody, unconscious girl with the ligature marks on her wrists that told the story of her torturous end.

They killed my mother, and then they killed my girl. My Juliette.

I think my father knew, then, when he returned from the hospital to tell me of her death, that I wouldn't cooperate with his fucking depravity anymore. I went wild. I beat him to a fucking pulp, and he let me, because I think he was reeling from the destruction he'd just enabled upon a girl he claimed to love as the daughter he'd never had.

His shock didn't last long, though. It quickly morphed into how to make my punishment most fitting for betraying my brotherhood and trying to get out with Juliette.

My father locked me away for three years after he killed Julz.

Three. Fucking. Years.

There's a house—a walled, gated compound, actually—on the north side of the American / Mexican border my grandfather owned. When I awoke, after my father told me Julz was dead and then tasered me, I was in a nine-by-nine foot cell, smooth limestone walls that would become my only companion.

My father visited me every day at the beginning. Together with my eldest brother, Chad, he gagged me with one of my socks and tied me to a chair, in front of a table that held a small TV and VCR.

My father, his face grim and set with determination, made Chad leave once I was secured. I struggled against my ropes as my father brought a girl in, dressed like a hooker in tight shorts and a strapless bodice thing that pushed her tits up and together. Her name was Starla, I remember, because she took that strapless thing off, and her shorts, until she was completely naked save for gold stars pasted onto her nipples.

I'd just watched my girlfriend be raped and murdered by my family, and I was in catatonia. Even if I'd wanted to be turned on, which I didn't, my body didn't even register that a naked chick was standing in front of me.

Not.One.Iota.

She looked around, a little unsure, until her eyes landed on my father.

"I'm not sure about this ..." she said slowly.

Dornan chuckled, pulled a gun out of his waistband and held it to her temple.

"Get sure," he snapped. Her eyes went wide, as they do when you hold a gun to somebody's head. I watched on, detached from their interaction, as though I wasn't even there. Even then, even before the depravity of the hole, I was already beginning to go insane.

I closed my eyes as she knelt between my open knees, her trembling hands reached for my belt buckle, opening it, unzipping my pants.

No.

Suddenly, the room was filled with the blaring of a girl's unmistakable screams. A girl begging. My eyes flew open, and I nearly choked on the fucking sock in my mouth as I saw what horror was unfolding on the screen in front of me.

I'd been so fixated on stopping my brothers from attacking Juliette that I'd barely noticed my father recording the entire thing.

And now he was playing back her brutal rape, for me to watch, while a girl knelt in front of me and reached into my pants.

When the video came on, she jumped, pulling away from me as the sound of Juliette's anguished sobs filled the small room. *Thank God*, I remember thinking as she recoiled from me. I knew she'd been reaching for my cock, and I couldn't bear the thought of her touching me, video or no video.

I closed my eyes and roared around the sock in my mouth, thinking that at least if I could make enough noise, at least if I could close my eyes and retreat somewhere safer inside my mind, that I wouldn't have to hear Juliette screaming for my brothers to stop.

Something hard and metal smacked against the back of my head. I opened my eyes reflexively as I felt warm blood ooze from my scalp. My father stood over me, having just pistol-whipped me across my skull, and over the video I heard the click of him cocking his revolver as he placed it against the girl's head. With his other hand he fisted her hair, dragging her back to her knees in front of me.

"Do it," he growled. "Get him off. Or I'll shoot you in the fuckin' face and leave you down here with him to rot."

She started to cry. No doubt she'd been picturing something a little easier when she agreed to come down and blow a Gypsy Brother.

I still remember how cold her fingers were when she grabbed my cock and brought it out into the air.

"Suck," Dornan commanded.

My senses were on overload. There was the cold hands on my cock and her hot breath and the video and the fucking gun, and I didn't know what to do.

Her mouth on my cock was revolting. It was like a leech, sucking on me. There was no pleasure. My body didn't even begin to respond to her. My cock stayed limp, despite her best efforts, the way she used her hands and mouth and tits to try and turn me on. She cried the whole time, her tears only making my cock slide in and out of her mouth with greater ease, but I stayed limp, because what the fuck was there to be turned on about?

After what seemed like forever, she stopped; I heard a pop as she released my soft cock from between her lips.

"I just want to leave," she said to my father. "I promise I won't tell anyone."

"No. Keep going."

She tried again, pulling out all of her best tricks. She tried to straddle me, to fuck me, but my cock was too useless for her to even maneuver it inside herself. And all the while, the video played in front of us, a ghastly backdrop for the punishment being meted out.

"It's not working!" the girl hissed at my father. "Please, don't make me keep going. He doesn't want it."

I was shaking. Vibrating. All I could hear was the pulse of my own blood in my ears as my heart thundered along, trying to protect me from the recorded sound of Juliette's pleas.

My father sighed. "Fine. But I'm not paying you. You didn't finish the job."

As he left the room with the girl, her mascara all over her pale face and her hair mussed up, I was still thinking that I'd be able to wait him out. That I'd never fall into his madness.

Then the girl screamed, a gunshot rang out, and something heavy hit the ground on the other side of the door.

He came back into the room, stepping over her dead, naked body to do so. I still remember the way the stars she'd pasted over her nipples glinted in the harsh fluorescent light that hung in the hallway.

"It's so hard to find decent help these days," my father said, reaching down and pulling the sock from my mouth as he laughed.

"Why?" I cried. "You didn't even know her!"

"It was never about her. It's about you. You will obey me, Jason," he said calmly. "You will obey me because I'm your father."

"I don't want to be your son!" I roared, and he smiled.

"You will," he said. "When you realize your only way out of here is to start acting like my son, you'll want me to be your father."

"I'll never call you my father. *Never*."

His dark eyes bored into me as I tried to forget the dead girl in the hallway, her blood puddling underneath her and spreading until it was almost at my toes.

"You think I won't break you," Dornan murmured, "But I'm a very patient man."

The next day I watched the video, pretended I was somewhere else, and groaned in agony as my balls screamed in pain and I came inside the girl who'd been bouncing on my red-raw cock for over an hour.

It wasn't pleasurable.

It wasn't good.

It was a fucking nightmare, one that would be repeated daily, for three years, until I stopped resisting and started fucking and choking every single girl that passed into the dark hole I was imprisoned in.

But that didn't matter to my father.

All that mattered was that I learned to obey.

All that mattered was that I learned to be his son.

CHAPTER SEVEN

Elliot

I love Juliette, but I fucking hate her right now, too.

But really, I can only blame myself, can't I? I'm the one who went along with her plans, back in the beginning when she was winning against the Gypsy Brothers. When she was cutting them down, one by one. I protested at every turn, but I'm no innocent bystander in all of this. I was a willing accomplice. I got her the drugs that killed Maxi. I personally crafted the multiple dirty bombs that she used to kill two brothers and injure two more. I told her she had to stop, and then I handed her everything she needed to keep going until she ended every one of those motherfuckers.

And now, we're in the aftermath. We're fucked, to put it plainly. Amy hates me, my little girl is turning into a freaking basket case, and the DEA is riding my ass to work for them in exchange for the 'favor' they did for all of us in Furnace Creek. The favor that cost us all our freedom. Juliette and Jase are lethal, but they're obviously too volatile, because all the DEA wants from them is their testimony against Julian Ross and the Gypsy Brothers MC. They're not asking them to join the ranks of law enforcement. No, they're just trying to make sure Juliette doesn't get an itchy trigger finger and find the remaining Gypsy Brothers just so she can waste them all.

This.Case.Is.Massive.

And once the DEA's done dismantling the Il Sangue Cartel and the Gypsy Brothers MC, they'll toss us all aside like garbage. As it is, they're not even offering protection to us, hence having to keep moving around every fucking five minutes.

I like to think I'm a pretty easygoing guy, but even I have my limit. And I'm afraid to say, I'm just about there. I'm so ready to walk into the DEA office and start shooting.

The only reason I don't is because they're the best shot any of us have at making it out of this mess alive.

Almost on cue, my cellphone rings. At first I don't recognize it as mine, because we're always changing our goddamn cellphones to evade being tracked. I'm standing in the shitbox kitchen of Jase and Juliette's apartment, watching as a fat cockroach makes its way up the wall. I tilt my head to the side, taking a newspaper from the dining table without breaking my gaze.

Thwack! I smash the dirty little fucker with the end of the rolled-up newspaper and smile, victorious. If only killing the rest of the Il Sangue Cartel was that easy. I hear movement behind me and spin around, the dirty bug forgotten as a gun is pointed at my face.

"Jesus!" Juliette says, lowering the gun to her side. I resist the urge to crack a joke, because her eyes are puffy and it's obvious she's been crying her fucking eyes out. Again. Is it bad that I'm secretly hoping her vengeful, kick-ass bitch side returns? Because this weepy girl with a vacant stare is not doing it for me.

"I almost shot you," Juliette says, placing her gun on the dining table.

"Jase asked me to stop by," I say, spreading my arms wide. The girl looks like she needs a fucking hug, and about sixteen fatty cheeseburgers injected right into her veins. Her jeans and black t-shirt are hanging off her slight frame, her cheekbones jutting out, her skin pale. She's a garish caricature of Juliette and Samantha, with her natural green eyes and her decidedly not natural nose and chest.

She doesn't hesitate. She tucks herself in underneath my chin, wrapping her skinny arms around my waist, and I squeeze her, not enough to take her breath away, but enough so that she knows she's being hugged. I'm a great hugger. I pride myself on my ability to hug-tackle women all over the country. Ha.

"How you doing, J girl?" One of my old nicknames for her.

I hear her draw in a hiccupped breath, and my face falls. She's crying. She's always crying. I've never seen her like this.

"Hey," I whisper, stroking her bright red hair with one hand, still damp from the shower she was taking when I arrived and Jase bolted. I'm still not used to the color, bright red and garish, but I guess that's the point. She looks nothing like the tanned brunette the Gypsies are searching for. As far as appearances go, I'd say she's fitting in just fine to the seediest stretch of Miami highway.

She disentangles herself from my embrace and wipes her eyes. "I'm sorry," she says, composing herself. "You must be so sick of seeing me like this."

"It's getting kind of old," I say, winking at her. She laughs, and that makes my heart happy.

We haven't been together for almost four years, but yeah. I'd do just about anything to bring the light back into this girl's green eyes.

"Jase gone?" she asks, staring at the door. I nod, taking her elbow and steering her towards the crappy sofa that looks like a breeding ground for lice and bacteria. It smells like wet dog in this apartment, and I can't help but wonder why they chose this dump to stay in after the palatial mansions they'd been accustomed to hiding out in.

Blending in, Jase told me. And he has a point, I guess. All of us—them and us—have survived and managed to stay hidden longer here than we have anywhere else.

"I brought you coffee," I say, handing Juliette the unmarked decaf latte from the tray on the coffee table in front of us. She's so amped up, she doesn't need a drop more adrenalin in her veins. Don't want her giving me attitude for it either, so it's secret decaf.

"Thank you," she says, taking the cup from me and drinking from it like it's the nectar of the gods or something. Seriously, she chugs about half of the Venti latte while I'm dumping packets of sugar in my own black coffee.

She stops to take a breath and smiles. "Decaf?"

She's too fucking smart. I feign shock. "I would *never.*"

"Ha ha," she says, setting the cup down in front of us. "Did Jase say where he was going?"

I shake my head. "Something about needing to meet with Fitz?"

Agent Fitzsimmons is our DEA handler. He's the one running intel between Jase, Julz, myself and the agency. Tommy's been pulled off the case and relegated to a desk job somewhere in the northwest, punishment for letting Juliette kill Dornan and Donny instead of arresting them and bringing them to trial. He didn't even try to stop her, and they know that. So, no more Tommy. We have this Fitz dude, or as I like to call him, "Fitzfucker".

Juliette's smile is gone now, replaced with a blank stare. "I haven't left this apartment since we arrived," she says. "I know he's just trying to protect me, but it feels like …" She trails off, her eyes widening as if she's afraid she's said too much.

"Feels like what?"

"Nothing," she says, "Never mind. How are the girls?"

I nod. "OK, considering." Amy's suffering from her own case of claustrophobia, but at least the place we're staying at doesn't have roaches the size of my fist crawling the walls. The house we're staying at is actually pretty nice, except for the part where we don't dare leave for fear of being shot on the front steps. Luis is there with the girls now, because I'm just like Jase—I refuse to leave them alone for one millisecond. It drives Amy nuts—strait-laced, career-driven, independent Ames is dying inside four walls. She's patient, though. She understands. After the terrifying forty-eight hours that Dornan held her and our daughter captive in Furnace Creek, Amy's willing to bear the frustration of me watching her like a hawk around the clock.

I still remember the way my gut twisted when the Gypsy Brothers took my girls. My little Kayla wasn't even three years old. Amy, as a psychologist employed by the LAPD, was used to sitting and listening to cops talk about discharging their guns, or seeing dead bodies. That kind of shit. She got to sit in an air-conditioned office and listen to the good guys unburden their secrets and fears, and then she got to go home at night to a safe place.

I took that safety away from her when I got involved with Juliette's vendetta against Dornan and his club. She became a target. That's on me.

Grandma hadn't been answering her phone, and my gut told me something was up. Then somebody burned my fucking tattoo shop on Venice Boulevard to the ground, somebody working for Dornan. I took that as a sign. Packed Amy and Kayla up, got them into my car, and hightailed it out of LA. The moment I'd seen the ashes of my tattoo shop, I knew why Grandma hadn't been picking up her phone. Because she was already compromised. *Because she was already dead.*

We drove to Nebraska. Kayla was freaking out—she was so little, so scared, and suddenly we were running. I forgot to pack her fucking teddy bear, and she cried and cried, for hours. I hadn't even packed food, or milk, just a couple of liter bottles of water for the three of us. Amy had some animal crackers in her handbag—I'd grabbed her straight from work after I collected Kayla from the sitter—but Kayla was beside herself after a few hours of driving.

I stopped at a gas station near Grandma's house to get her milk and a new teddy. I was out of the car for thirty seconds when they pulled up and stole my car, stole my girls from the parking lot of a Quik Stop.

I still remember how I dropped the carton of milk on the ground, the way it exploded at my feet. I dropped the teddy bear, too, in a puddle of oil, just as my car disappeared into traffic.

Dornan Ross had my girls.

I got them back—after an excruciating couple of days—but I didn't make it to Grandma in time, and even though the little voice inside my head blames Julz, I'm the one who fucked up.

"Where do you think he goes?" Juliette asks me. "Do you think he's meeting Fitzsimmons?" She looks so young, her face scrubbed of any makeup, her eyes full of everything that troubles her. *And there are so many things.* She's like a ghost of two girls—Juliette Portland and Samantha Peyton—because she's both of those people, and she's neither. She's what was left behind after the fall.

"Sure." I shrug, tiny alarm bells ringing in the back of my head. "Where else would he be?"

She just stares straight through me, chewing on her thumbnail.

"He still won't tell me what happened to him while I was in Nebraska with you all those years," she says finally. "He won't tell, and I know it was bad. I wish he would tell me. I wish he would *trust* me."

I shift awkwardly, and she catches my expression with lightning speed. "Did he tell you?" she asks. "Do you know?"

"Whoa," I say. "Steady on, cowgirl. While you were—" *Jesus, how do I even put it?* "—missing, Jase told me a couple things about his time in the hole. Nothing concrete. No details. Just that he was down there for a very long time, and you already know that."

He told me more. Not a lot more, but more than I'd be willing to tell Juliette right now. I love the girl, but he trusted me with his secrets, with his shame, and I'm not about to break that trust. Some fucked up things happened, and he should be the one to tell her, not me. She'll just have to ask him herself. And keep asking, until he tells her.

"He must have told you something," Juliette says, chewing her bottom lip.

"Julz."

"*El*."

I sigh, remembering the shaky way Jase had recounted his own captivity as we searched for Juliette together. "He told me it was dark. That it was always dark."

She breathes in sharply, covering her mouth with her palm. Her eyes spill over as she holds the other hand to her flat stomach, folding over onto herself until her face is pressed up against her knees. She's saying something over and over again, but I can't hear what the words are, because she's saying them into her knees, and the sound is muffled.

I frown, focusing on the words, putting my hand on her back when I finally figure out what she's saying.

HeLeftTheLightsOnForMe

Hate rises in my throat, bitter and raw, as I try not to imagine what she went through. What they both went through. One in the light, one in the dark.

Dornan might be dead, but he's still managing to fuck with these two—with all of us—from the grave.

CHAPTER EIGHT

Jase

So I wasn't meeting with Agent Fitzsimmons. I lied to Elliot when he asked where I was going. I'm blocks away, pacing in an alleyway as I speak to Tommy on my burner phone.

"I've got a bad feeling about this motherfucker, Tommy," I say, eyeing off the crumbling red bricks in front of me. I make a fist. Think briefly about punching the wall. Decide, reluctantly, that I don't need the questions my bloodied knuckles might raise. God, I can't even take out my rage on an inanimate fucking object without being hassled these days.

I.Am.Suffocating.Here.

I fucking hate this place.

"You and me both," Tommy replies. "My gut says he's dirty."

I roll my eyes. Our DEA handler might be dirty, but until we can prove something, we're at his whim. One wrong move—one attempt to move without their permission—and Juliette and I will be thrown in jail, the murder rap the CIA brought upon us reinstated automatically. The DEA are helping us stay hidden, and for now that's the lesser of two evils. Juliette cannot go to prison. My grandfather's cartel will have her killed in her cell before she so much as tastes her first prison meal.

"Where are you?" I ask Tommy. "Why aren't you here, man?"

Tommy snorts. "I'm in San *fucking* Fran, dude. Don't tell Fitzsimmons you know that. I'm meant to be off the grid."

I kick at the broken asphalt with my boot tip. Too fucking hot in Miami to wear jeans and boots, but it's kind of hard to conceal a Glock in shorts. I wipe the thin sheen of sweat from my forehead, and it springs back instantly. I hate this place so goddamn much. I'd gladly suffer through the dry Californian heat any day, but this humidity shit is fucking ridiculous. It feels like I'm being dragged through quicksand every time I step out of that shitty apartment.

"San fucking Fran? What the hell kind of crime even happens there? iPad theft?"

"Ha ha," Tommy says dryly. "You'd be surprised. We've got our own drug cartel to deal with up here. Fucking Russian pricks. Seems your granddaddy has associates in Frisco."

"Really," I say. "You know people there hate it when you call it Frisco. Or San Fran."

"No shit," Tommy says, chuckling. "I called it GeekTown in a meeting the other day. Should have seen their faces. I can't help it if I'm a badass biker from Venice Beach."

"Right. So, can you get me anything on this Fitz guy? I'm gonna have to shoot him if he keeps fucking around."

I hear a spitting noise. "Do NOT shoot him!" Tommy says.

"Relax, brother. I was joking." It's funny how neither of us are technically Gypsy Brothers anymore, because he's MIA and I'm being hunted down, but he's more of a brother to me than any of my flesh and blood brothers ever were.

"Ahh, shit, man!" he says. "I just spat coffee all over my fucking MacBook! It's a gold plated one. Do you know how long I had to stand in line to get this?"

I roll my eyes. "Are you sure you're not gay, Tommy? No judgement here. But really. A gold MacBook?"

I hear him sip his coffee again and decide it can't be that bad.

"I'm not gay," Tommy says, and I hear him rummaging in the background. "I met a lovely girl, I'll have you know. She's a massage therapist."

"She give you a happy ending?" I quip, not to be an asshole, but because it's so fucking refreshing to just talk to somebody half normal.

"Not until the second date," Tommy replies. "She said I had the softest feet."

"I don't even know what to say to that, Tommy."

He laughs. "Right. I gotta go. This laptop is all I've got to watch Busty Brazilian Beauties on, and you've just sizzled the fucking thing."

"Stick it in a bag of rice or something," I say dismissively, ending the call. We're talking about getting murdered here, and he's worried about spilling coffee on his shiny new laptop. Still, at the same time, his flippant nature makes the burden of my existence a fraction easier to bear.

Once I get back to the apartment, the momentary lapse of constant tension is shattered—along with Juliette, who looks like she needs a paper bag to breathe into and some Xanax to calm her the fuck down. Hell, a shot of vodka. Anything. She's sitting on the couch with Elliot, and when I open the front door, she's pointing her gun at me.

I raise my eyebrows, and she puts the gun down, wiping her eyes with her fingers. I immediately regret leaving her after I fucked her on the bed, but I needed to get away before I did something I seriously regretted. Like tried to choke her, or tied her up and spanked the shit out of her, or pushed her down to her knees and fucked her mouth until she begged me to stop. I can't do those things to her, because she's my girl, and I love her, and I *shouldn't want to do those things to her*. It might be okay to other people—fuck, there are entire lifestyles built around dominating somebody sexually—but it's Juliette, and after what my father did to her, after what *all of them* did to her, I can't be rough with her. I can't bring violence to our bed, to our relationship. I see the way Elliot is with her—effortlessly tender, gentle, patient—and I have no fucking idea how to be that person. I try. I try so fucking hard to be the man she needs me to be. But it's getting harder. I've got this rage inside me that never lets up, and I need somewhere for it to go.

"What'd I miss?" I ask, looking from Elliot to Juliette.

Elliot shrugs. "Just Netflix and chill, you know?"

I snort. "You know what that means, right?"

Elliot laughs. "Yeah. Just wanted to see the look on your face. You look like you could use a laugh or two. You're gonna get wrinkles if you keep frowning like that, you know." He scrunches his face up dramatically and I shake my head. I don't know how Tommy and Elliot can be so fucking cheery all the time. Even when we're at what seems like the world's end, and even though Elliot's got a *kid* in the fray, he can still crack jokes as fast as I can blink.

"Hey, if we could get Netflix on that piece of shit TV, I'd move in permanently."

"Well, you missed an excellent episode of *Sally Jesse Raphael*," Elliot responds cheerily, gesturing to the rerun flickering on the tired television. "You're just in time for *Oprah*, though."

I grab a beer from the kitchen and pop the lid off, tossing it in the trash as I take a long gulp. I hold the bottle up at Elliot, and he shakes his head. Deflated, I take one more gulp and tip the rest of the beer down the sink. I can't be slowed down. Man, how I'd love to just relax and drink a fucking beer, but there's not much point in trying to breathe in this hellish existence we're in the middle of right now. I need to be sharp. On my toes. Twenty-four-fucking-seven.

"What'd I miss?" I repeat, my focus flipping between them. Julz shakes her head and wipes her eyes again. Elliot shrugs. I fight the urge to roll my eyes and walk past them, heading out to the tiny balcony where I can smoke.

Yeah. I'm smoking again. I haven't smoked in years, but it's something to do with my hands, something to occupy the idle hours. There's something so raw and satisfying about burning yourself black from the inside out, and so yeah, I'm smoking again.

I light up, thinking about Fitzsimmons. I don't trust him as far as I can throw him. I want the other girl back, the first DEA agent who approached me three years ago, when I'd just been freshly evicted from my dungeon at Emilio's and back into society. But she's not even DEA anymore. I think she's FBI, if Tommy's queries were anything concrete. She's FBI, and we're stuck with Fitzfucker, who I don't trust.

After I've taken a few drags of my Marlboro, the harsh smoke settling into my lungs like an old friend, I hear the screen door open and close. I don't turn. It'll either be Juliette, asking me questions, or Elliot, asking me questions. Whoever it is, they'll be asking me the same fucking questions. I'm leaning against the lip of the balcony, looking into the dirty canals, wondering where I'd dump a body if I needed to.

"How'd it go?"

Juliette.

I turn my head as she settles in beside me, her elbows balanced on the side of the balcony. She's got her bright red locks pulled up into a messy bun, and she's put makeup on while I was gone. Heavy eyeliner and mascara that make her green eyes stand out, especially with the hair. She's fucking beautiful, and she's mine, and I can't bear the sight of her.

I shrug. "Nothing new." I'm not lying, technically. I didn't find out anything new. She doesn't need to know that I didn't meet with anyone. If I talk too much about my suspicions—that I think the DEA is going to sacrifice us in this trial—I think her anxiety will get so bad, I won't be able to help her come back down to reality again. She's on the brink of madness, and something like this could be the thing that makes her fall.

She plucks the cigarette from my lips and places it in hers, her lips so fucking sexy when she sucks, inhaling the same poison I've just been breathing in. It's a perfect fucking metaphor for our relationship; I'm poisoning her a little bit more each day. She doesn't even know it. She thinks I forgave her for everything she's done—fucking me and my father at the same time, running away from me back in Santa Monica, lying to me about her drug addiction and losing our baby in a haze of brutal heroin comedown—because I'm a nice person.

When really, I forgave her because I've done so much worse. And she thinks I'm her light, but I'm her worst fucking nightmare.

She passes the cigarette back to me, and I look out to the canals, dirty, dark water the perfect breeding ground for sharks. There are signs everywhere: BEWARE THE MANATEES, but it's the sharks I'd be more worried about.

"Have I done something to make you angry?" Julz asks in a small voice, and I sigh. Turn to her, pulling her into me. Every man in her life has either abused her, let her down, or just plain fucking left, and I have to remind myself to get out of my own damned head and be there for her like she needs.

"No, baby," I say, hugging her so tight I can feel her ribs. "I'm just tired of this fucking place."

I feel her head nod beneath my chin. "Me too," she whispers. "I just want to go home."

I kiss the top of her head, as she adds wryly, "I just wish we had a home."

I put my hands on her shoulders and pull her back so I can see her face; those green, glassy eyes will be the death of me. "Baby," I say, softening, squeezing her to my chest again. I put the cigarette between my teeth so I can use both of my hands to grip her slight frame to mine, to make her feel safe, to make her feel like she's still mine. I'm so fucking angry with myself for the way I left her on the bed with my come all over her. She thinks I was gone when she started crying, but I heard the first sob before she muffled herself.

I fucked her, and left her, and made her cry. I'm a fucking bastard.

"We'll have a home. Wherever you want. Colorado, or LA, or fucking Antarctica. When this is all over we'll be free."

When you're dead you're free, right? Eternal freedom. Except we're probably going to hell to hang out with Daddy Dornan. I don't tell her that, though. I don't tell her that for the first time, I'm not sure if we're going to make it out of this alive. I know she feels that way too, and I know that more than anything, she needs me to be her voice of hope.

"I wish we hadn't buried her," she whispers against my chest, and I stiffen at the mention of our baby. I suck on the cigarette between my teeth, savoring the dirty smoke that comes with air, a physical destruction from the hammer that's shattering my heart into tiny shards. I hate talking about our daughter. It just makes me remember all over again, every minute of that day in a fucking loop. The argument Julz and I had. The bright blood on her white panties, the way she touched a hand to herself and brought it away red, almost in slow motion. The way I held her as I raced to the fucking hospital, not knowing if either of them would survive.

I don't want to remember everything that we lost that day, but it's all she wants to talk about. I think Juliette's afraid if we stop talking about our baby, it will be like it never happened, even though it's all I think about. I'm young, and I'm a fucking loose cannon, but I was somebody's father for a moment there, and in that moment, I saw all the good things I could have been.

There's no good left, and I don't want to fucking talk about it.

I have to agree with her, though. I wish we hadn't buried her ashes in Colorado, because we're getting further away, and even though our daughter's dead and it doesn't make sense, I want to be near her. I want to brush the snow from her grave and take fresh flowers. I want to carry her with us, always.

We're so fucking far away.

"Me too," I say, my throat painfully tight, my fists clenched. I take the cigarette from my mouth and drop it, smashing it beneath my boot as the sun pounds down onto us. Even the sunshine here feels grimy, and that's coming from someone who lives in dirty Los Angeles.

"We never named her," Julz says, the side of her face still squashed against my chest, probably listening to make sure my heart's still beating and I'm not completely dead inside.

I stroke her hair, marveling at how the color change hasn't taken away from the feel. It feels—and smells—just like it did the first time I touched it, when she was fourteen and blonde and I was just a boy. It smells like vanilla and feels like silk. I love her. I don't fucking deserve her.

"We didn't," I agree. "No name ever seemed good enough. No name was perfect."

"That's how I feel, too," Julz says, her voice oddly calm. Usually she's crying when we talk about this. It's a relief, to hear her able to speak without crying for once. Because when she cries, I just want to run out into the street, gun drawn, and start shooting motherfuckers until she stops crying. Problem is, the right motherfuckers aren't here for me to shoot.

"No name was ever good enough," I repeat. "She was just ours. And we loved her. And that's all that matters."

Julz pulls back, the ghost of a smile on her mouth as she reaches her hand up, brushing her thumb across my lower lip.

"Where'd your name come from?" she asks me. I shrug, because I honestly don't know. "I just know my mom picked it for me."

"I never asked my mom why she picked Juliette," Julz says, and my blood runs cold in my veins. *That's because she didn't name you*, I think, trying to compose my face. But Julz … Jesus Christ, she's sharp. She can read me like a fucking book.

My father told me the story of Juliette's birth one day. He wasn't always horrid to me. Most of the time he was, but after I'd been down there a while, he would visit sporadically with a couple beers and just … talk. He always had a gun, so it's not like I could stop him. He was always in control. But; *yeah*. When you haven't spoken to someone in weeks, and then your psychopathic father comes for bonding time with you, it's pretty fucking weird.

Anyway. He told me about Juliette's birth. How her mother had been so fucking high, she couldn't even name her own kid. How he'd always wanted a daughter, but how, after all sons, he'd realized that was never going to happen. How he'd always liked the name Juliette.

And as all this is flashing before my eyes, the cogs in Juliette's brain are drawing lines and connecting dots and firing fucking synapses. I glance to my left, watching Elliot as he paces inside the apartment, talking on his cellphone. Great. I can just tell that as soon as I'm done destroying Juliette's soul a little more out here, I'll be hearing some bad fucking news in *there*.

"Emilio's brother is called Julian," she says, and I snap my gaze back to her as she steps back from me. "You don't think—"

"No," I say too quickly. Goddamn it. She's shrewd, even when she's kind of crazy. Her green eyes stare at me, full of questions, full of suspicion. God, I'm a bad liar. To her, at least.

"No secrets," she whispers. "Remember? We don't keep secrets. No secrets."

The way she keeps repeating herself freaks me the fuck out. I mean, I'm no doctor, but *something's wrong with my girl.* I feel it. I see it, in the way she zones out. The way she has to line up everything in perfect synchronicity—our toothbrushes, our shoes, the threadbare sheets that wrap around our temporary bed. Everything must line up perfectly. And the way she watches me, when she thinks I'm not looking. The way she looks at me like I'm something frightening. She never used to look at me like that.

She looks at me the way she looked at *him* in those moments before he shot me. Utter terror. Like she's made of glass, and if I look at her front-on, she'll smash into a million bloody shards at my feet.

Pity she can't line up the broken pieces of her soul. Or mine.

"Dornan named you," I confess, because I can't lie to her. Because I promised I'd never lie to her. Because she deserves to know. Dornan named her. *The daughter he never had. The vessel for all of his rage. Juliette.* "Your mom took off after she had you. She didn't give you a name. Your dad was in solitary confinement in prison. The birth certificate needed a name."

Dornan named her, and now she knows.

Her eyes go wide for a second. That's it. That's the only reaction she has. She doesn't cry. Doesn't gasp. She.Does.Nothing.

"Julz," I say, "It doesn't mean anything."

Elliot chooses that exact fucking moment to step out onto the small balcony, so small that we barely fit. I glance at him, his mouth open and his cellphone still lit up in his hand, and my eyes must tell him to shut the fuck up, because he closes his mouth again and looks from me to Juliette.

"He killed me. Did I tell you that?" Her face is blank, so utterly vacant I'm the one who's terrified. "He killed me and brought me back, over and over again."

"What?" I say. "What are you talking about?"

"Guys—" Elliot interjects.

"Shut up," I snap at him. "Let her talk."

I don't want to hear. I don't want to know. But I have to know.

She looks from me to Elliot and back again, rubbing a spot on the top of her arm, finally turning her gaze to the ugly canals below us.

"He had this stuff that he'd inject, into my arm," she murmurs. "Or my neck, or sometimes my thigh. It hurt. After a while, I stopped feeling where he put the needle, because it didn't matter, everything was just pain. He'd put one needle in and I'd stop breathing, and everything would go dark, and just as the pain was fading away he'd put something else in the needle to wake me up again. He was stopping my heart and starting it again. He was killing me and bringing me back."

I remember how I felt when Dornan shot me in the chest, when everything went cold and I was bleeding out on the ground between him and Julz. I glance at Elliot, his jaw clenched, his eyes bloodshot, and I bet that's what he's remembering, too. He and I both almost died by Dornan's hand that day, a bullet each for our treachery, and I imagine what Juliette had to go through waking up alive and knowing he was going to do it to her all over again.

Juliette swallows thickly, looking so small, so alone. "And then he'd tie me to the bed and take his clothes off and push inside me—"

No.

"—and I'd cry because I was so fucking ashamed that I wanted him to rape me instead of putting those needles in me, because at least it felt better than *dying.*"

I clench my fists until I feel bone crunch on itself, every muscle in my body coiled and ready for attack. I imagine Julz naked and bound, her legs tied to rusted bedposts, being fucked, enjoying it. *No.* I want to tear someone apart, to feel their fucking life drain away between my hands as I squeeze every drop of life out of them. I remember the way I took Donny's knife and butchered him, my own brother, hacked and stabbed and cut until he was unrecognizable and it felt like I was drowning in his blood.

I want to do that to someone now. I want to do that to Dornan. But I can't because he's dead, and we're hiding, and there's nowhere else to go.

I can't help it; my rage screams to a boil inside me, and something has to come out. I smash one of my fists into the wall, feeling the way my bones protest, cracking under the weight of my fatal desire. I want to kill him. I want to kill them all.

Julz doesn't even react.

Her eyes fill with tears, now, her eyes on me.

"He named me?"

I wish to God that I'd lied to her.

"Guys," Elliot says again, his tone sharper this time. "We've been made. Cartel knows we're in Miami. We're leaving. We have to go. *Now.*"

CHAPTER NINE

Juliette

"And go where?" I ask Elliot incredulously, watching the way Jase's knuckles drip with blood. "There's nowhere left to go. Everywhere we go, they find us."

I look out towards the ocean, where storm clouds are gathering, like they do almost every afternoon at some point. Fucking Florida. I never thought I'd say that I miss LA, but *I fucking miss LA* and its reliable sunshine.

"Back to California," Elliot says. "Fuck this DEA bullshit. I'm going, Luis is going, and Tommy's meeting us there. This is a war, and it's time to stop pansying around and make shit happen. Since when have either of you cared about immunity? About following orders? How about *never*? But, hey, if you two want to stay here and talk about *Daddy fucking Dornan* and get killed? Be.My.Guest. But I'm betting you want a one-way ticket back to LA with me. So grab your shit, or we're all going back in body bags."

The body bag comment gets Jase and I moving. I've already got my gun shoved in the back of my jeans, easily accessible at a moment's notice. We haul ass into the tiny apartment, each grabbing our bag—one each, to hold a toothbrush, underwear, bullets, and water—and all three of us are out the door and in Elliot's rental car inside of ninety seconds. Jase and I shove into the backseat and Elliot takes the driver's seat. This isn't the first time we've had to move. It's becoming a blur now, it's happened so often.

Elliot guns the engine and dons a baseball cap, pulling it tight over his head so his face is obscured. As Jase and I check the clips in our guns, shrinking down low in the seats so we won't be seen, Elliot shrugs into a zippered navy blue hoodie, pulling the sleeves down to his wrists to cover his tattoos.

Without warning, we screech off, fishtailing as we pull onto Biscayne Boulevard. Elliot's always been a good driver, but the way he's weaving in and out of cars right now makes me want to puke. I reach over and squeeze Jase's hand. He seems surprised, but he looks back at me, gripping my hand tightly.

"What about Amy and Kayla?" I ask Elliot as he speeds down the highway.

"We're meeting them at the airstrip," Elliot says. "They're with Luis. And we've got—" he checks his watch—"an hour to get to the airstrip before our pilot goes back to LA without us. If we don't make it, at least the girls will. Tommy will meet them there."

"You think we won't make it?" I ask.

Elliot shakes his head tightly. I see the way his hands clutch the steering wheel, a death grip that's turning his fingers white. "We'll make it."

"Who was on the phone?" Jase asks Elliot.

"Tommy. He got a tip-off. Julian Ross is on his way to Miami."

There's that name again. *Julian.* Emilio's younger brother, Dornan's uncle. I cringe as it leaves Elliot's mouth. Then I remember that he didn't hear the conversation Jase and I just had about my name. That Elliot doesn't know what I've just been told. That Dornan chose my name. That he's been *choosing* for me since the day I was born. When I lived. When I died. When I suffered. And how, even though he's dead, he's still deciding for me.

"I just spoke to Tommy, like, half an hour ago," Jase says. "He was fine."

"You didn't tell me you spoke to him," I say, a strange feeling in my chest. It's odd that he wouldn't tell me they had spoken. I feel so left out of what's going on. So useless.

It makes me angry.

"I didn't meet with Fitzsimmons," Jase says. "I was talking to Tommy. Figuring out how to check on Fitz, see if he's dirty."

Elliot takes his cap off and slides his sleeves up, and I take that to mean we're far enough away from the motel block to be pretty safe. I sit up, looking out the window to see more palm trees and fucking canals.

"I'm calling Isobel," Jase says.

"The fuck is Isobel?" Elliot glances over his shoulder at Jase, saying what I'm thinking. A ripple of jealousy flares through my stomach, unbidden and completely unfair. I'm not allowed to be jealous. I fucked Jase's father for months, some of it while I was fucking him at the same time. Sometimes, I fucked them both on the same *day*. More than anyone, I have no right to be jealous.

"My old DEA handler," Jase says, flipping his phone open and scrolling through numbers.

"Old?" I echo. "What do you mean?"

"Before Fitz," Jase says, still not looking at me. "She switched to FBI. Wanted to stay near her family. The DEA kept sending her away on shitty cases. Plus, the DEA's fucked."

"You mean to say," Elliot interrupts him, "that you've had an FBI contact sitting on your phone this whole time, and you didn't tell us?"

Jase mumbles something unintelligible.

"What's wrong with you?" I ask. "Are you—are you blushing?"

His jaw tightens. "Since when do I fucking *blush*, Juliette?"

I lean away, my throat tight, my stomach churning. I feel like I've laid my soul bare, told him things I never wanted to tell anyone, and he won't give me *anything*. Not a thing. "How do we know she's trustworthy?" I ask. *Isobel.* Sounds like a pretty girl's name.

"Do you trust me?"

"Of course I trust you," I snap.

"Then trust me to know who's fucking trustworthy."

I shake my head, staring out of my window. Fuck Jase. Fuck Isobel, whoever she is. Fuck all of this.

Why won't he just tell me what happened to him while I was with Elliot in Nebraska?

I fold my arms across my chest and grit my teeth. I'm pissed. I don't like this, not one bit. At least when Dornan was alive I had some semblance of control. I knew what he liked, and I knew how to give it to him. I kept him sated. I kept him in the dark. Now, I'm the one who's being kept in the dark, about everything, and I'm fucking sick of it.

Jase makes the call. I hear a female voice on the other end pick up, but she doesn't speak loud enough for me to make out any words. Jase's tone is clipped, almost hurried. Like he can't wait to get off the phone to her. Like he's a nervous teenager. He details our situation to her and I see the visible relief on his face after he listens to what she's got to say. When he ends the call, Elliot turns to look at him, raising his eyebrows. "You gonna fill us in?"

Jase clears his throat. "She'll meet with me," he says. "Tonight. In LA."

"*Just* you?" I ask, my tone probably a little too acerbic.

"Just me," he repeats. "She's risking her job to come meet as it is."

"Were you with her?" I ask, the words escaping my mouth before I can clamp my dumb mouth shut.

Jase's eyebrows practically hit the fucking roof. "You mean how you were *with* Dornan? Yeah. I was with her. It was a long fucking time ago."

"Fuck you, Jason," I snap, my cheeks burning. I'm too angry at what he's said to form any more words. All I can think about is *Isobel* and Jase and how he was totally justified in what he just said to me.

"You two should think less about Dornan and more about getting out of this thing alive," Elliot interjects, his tone serious. "He's dead, remember? Think about everything you both went through to get here. What's the point if you're just going to be assholes to each other?"

Jase lets out a breath he's been holding, clenching and unclenching his bloodied fist. I shoot laser beams from my eyes into the back of Elliot's head and try not to scream. I want to get out of this car. I'm fucking dying in here.

Jase glances at me, his expression softening a little. I swallow thickly, a little thrill shooting down my spine. Those eyes. Fuck. I'd melt under that gaze. Elliot's right. We're being total fucking assholes to each other and we're all we've got. Self-destruction, a skill we both excel at.

"We were friends," Jase says. "It was a long, long time ago. You were *gone*. She needed me for her case, and I needed her to get Dornan locked down. That's all. Nobody knew you'd burst in like a fucking hurricane and start blowing shit up."

He says the last sentence like he's impressed I did that, the corner of his mouth twitching. I take a deep breath and let it out, my frayed nerves and my anger settling back down in my stomach.

Elliot glances at Jase in the rear-view mirror. "She pretty? She single?"

I lean over and smack Elliot's arm.

"What," he laughs, taking one hand off the steering wheel and putting it up in a defensive gesture. "I'm single, Julz. I've got to take what I can get. Do you think she'll go on a date with me?"

I smack him again as Jase smirks beside me. "Nobody is dating the FBI chick!"

"Are you trying to make me crash this car?" Elliot asks, pulling his shoulder away from where I'm whacking him. He's trying not to smile and failing dismally.

"What the fuck kind of car is this?" Jase asks, looking around. "This isn't a Mustang."

"Mustang's a little conspicuous," Elliot says. "I had it trucked to Tommy's place in San Francisco to store until this shit blows over. I can't have it getting smashed in a chase. Besides, do you know how easy it would be to spot?"

"God forbid we should go any faster in this *Taurus*," Jase says. Elliot responds by flooring it, making both Jase and I jerk back in our seats. I keep my eyes trained on our surroundings as they whizz past, noticing that we're getting closer to downtown with each mile. Airstrips aren't usually downtown, unless we're grabbing a helicopter out of here.

"Are you planning on smashing this car in a chase?" I ask dubiously.

Elliot shrugs. "Not so far. Depends if we get tailed."

I look at Jase, my eyebrows raised. I hope to fuck we don't get tailed.

His hand is still dripping blood, and I've got the sudden urge to wrap the edge of my shirt around his knuckles and apply pressure until the bleeding slows. I look back to his eyes, though, and they're uncertain. I think back to what we just spoke about—how I just bared my soul to the both of them—and I turn away, sinking back into my seat as Miami flashes past us outside. I think of the way he used to make love to me, compared to the way he did this morning, and I wonder if we'll make it out of this thing together.

CHAPTER TEN

Jase

Fuck my life.

No, seriously. I haven't spoken to Isobel in two fucking years, since she left the DEA, and now I'm seeing her tonight.

Last time I saw her I came all over her face and then left her tied up and naked in a private room inside The Black Heart.

She wants to meet at the same fucking club. With me. *Just* me. Nobody else.

Fuck my life.

I'd never, ever touch another woman, not when I've got Julz, but the thought of going back to the place where I freely indulged all my darkest desires is making my heart thump out of my fucking chest.

I don't want to go back there. The old me would be there quicker than lightning, but the old me was a psychopath. And shit, maybe I'm still a psychopath, but: Julz.

I can feel the insecurity rolling off her like flames licking at my skin. I was an asshole; shouldn't have said what I did about her and my father. But sometimes, I get so fucking angry about it all, I can't keep it inside.

I knew Julian would find us eventually—Julian or one of the Gypsies. Same thing, different fucking name. The Cartel and the MC are like parasitic twins that feed off each other, interchangeable. One travels on Harley Davidsons, the other in a fleet of slick black town cars with bulletproof windows and plenty of room for stowing bodies in the trunks. Dornan might be dead, and Emilio might be dead, the two power players, the two kingpins of the entire organization, but it doesn't matter. It never mattered. Fuck, we were so stupid. I really, truly believed that once my father was either dead or behind bars in maximum security, that life would finally begin.

I glance at Julz, who is playing with her engagement ring, the one I gave to her in Colombia when her stomach had just started to swell and she had that pregnancy glow in her cheeks. The band is too big for her—we never did find the time to have it resized—but she insists on wearing it anyway, and that makes me fucking proud. She's my girl. Despite everything, she's my girl, and she's still wearing my ring.

My eyes drop from her fingers to my own. My hand has finally stopped bleeding, the dull ache in my knuckles reminding me, throb by throb, of the story Juliette decided to share about being killed and brought back to life and fucking raped.

I think about what my father did to my mother. What he did to my girl.

I can't decide which one is worse.

CHAPTER ELEVEN

Juliette

We get to the airstrip with minutes to spare. I can see now what Elliot hasn't mentioned, the reason the plane is leaving with or without us—a giant motherfucking electrical storm barreling in over the ocean. I glare at the insidious clouds as they gather and darken, rolling towards us. I fucking hate this place. If I weren't running for my life maybe I'd enjoy a cocktail with one of those little umbrellas poolside, but when you're running for your life, thunderstorms delaying your flight are really fucking inconvenient.

Elliot parks and jumps out of the car and runs to the plane, Luis greeting him at the door. He points to the sky and I hear a loud rumble that reverberates all the way down to my toes, my senses going on high alert. Fuck this place. *Let's just get the hell out of here*, I think.

"You coming?" Jase asks, grabbing his bag and mine. I nod, feeling naked without anything to carry, my only possession the gun in my waistband. He slams his door shut, coming around to my side and yanking mine open. It's like the thunder and the sudden arrival have fried my brain. I'm moving like I'm stuck in quicksand.

"Let's go," Jase says, holding out his hand. I take it, letting him pull me from the car, and before I can marvel at his touch, he's pulled away again, falling into step beside me. I try not to let it mean anything, but it does. When we were young—before everything was ripped away—he'd hold my hand while it stormed.

"Juliette," he'd say, under the covers with me so I couldn't see the flashing lightning. "It's okay. It's beautiful. One day, you'll learn to watch it. It's just nature."

He'd distract me by kissing me, by wrapping his strong arms around me. He was my protector, even then, even before any of this.

We board the plane, an upscale Gulfstream that looks shiny and new. I pass the cockpit, where our pilot sits patiently, watching the horizon. Luis is the first face I see, and behind him, Elliot's already in the back, leaning over Amy as Kayla dozes on her lap.

Luis practically tackle-hugs me as I pass the small galley and step into the airplane's interior. The seats are arranged in two clusters of four, with an extra two seats at the rear, and one small bathroom at the very back. Luis hasn't changed a bit, with his shaved head, his dark blue eyes that remind me of Mariana's, and his low-slung jeans that look like they'll fall off at any moment.

"How you doing, *bebé*?" he murmurs. I shrug, giving him my most dazzling smile.

"That bad, huh?" He pats my cheek with his hand. "Try get some sleep on this flight. You're beautiful, but you look like shit."

I laugh. "Thanks, Luis."

The storm's picking up. I can hear the fucking thing outside. The wind is picking up, and a few drops of rain smack against the small round windows that line the cabin in two neat rows.

"Hey, we're all here, boss," Luis calls to the pilot. It's funny, because Luis is the boss here, and I still have no idea how he finances all this. I know he's got ties to the Skullz Cartel, but I'm not sure how high up he is.

I wave to Amy, and she smiles back politely. I'm fairly sure she doesn't like me at all, and I don't blame her one bit. She's been dragged into this shit because of me, and I'm actually surprised she hasn't been more openly hostile towards me. We've barely spoken two words to each other since we properly 'met' in the hospital after Elliot and Jase were shot by Dornan, and I'm pretty sure we won't be becoming besties any time soon. Because of the things I've done, she's had to leave her post as a psychologist with the LAPD and drag her daughter around the country. Not to mention that time she was taken hostage by Dornan Ross and threatened with death.

Yeah. I think it's wise if I sit up front and let her have all the space at the back of the plane.

I take the first seat that faces the cockpit, putting my back to the rest of the plane. I kick my duffel bag underneath my seat and watch out the window, making sure we aren't followed.

The sky cracks again and I stiffen, gripping my leather armrest. I hate flying. I hate storms. Right now I just want to be on the ground, in a dimly lit room, huddled in the corner so I can rock back and forth for a few months, undisturbed.

I feel the seat beside me shift and look over to see Elliot. I crane my neck past him, seeing Jase next to Amy, chatting to her and Luis.

"You never told me about that," Elliot says. "What you said back at the apartment …" He trails off.

"I never told anyone," I said. "It's not exactly dinner-table conversation."

"Oh, because we're sitting at the dinner table so often together," Elliot says, mocking me.

I smile into my lap. *Let's go, let's get out of here*. I fidget with my seatbelt, making sure it's pulled tight. I tuck my hair behind my ears. Play with my armrests. All while feeling the questioning eyes of one Elliot McRae as he sits beside me, probably pondering his next sentence.

"Something on your mind, El?" I ask pointedly. I don't look at him. I don't want him to see all the bad things inside me.

"What'd you mean when you said he named you?" he asks, his words rushed as they spill out. Huh. I hadn't expected that. I take a deep breath and raise my eyes to meet his.

"They needed a name for my birth certificate," I say calmly, feeling anything but calm inside. "Dornan chose Juliette. The name he was going to use if he ever had a daughter."

Elliot sags in his seat. "Fuck."

Even my name isn't mine.

I liked my name. Juliette, like Shakespeare's, but with a couple more letters. Star-crossed lovers. Juliet and Romeo. Juliette and Jason.

I was named after someone who wants me dead.

Named by someone who almost destroyed me.

I don't even know who I am anymore.

Fuck," I echo limply. "That's definitely the word for it."

"It doesn't mean anything," Elliot says. "It doesn't."

"I don't like it here," I whisper, fully realizing that I sound just like a child as I look over at Elliot. "It storms too fucking much. It scares me."

Elliot softens, his expression neutral. I can tell he's struggling to maintain his poker face. He's worried about me. They're all so worried about crazy little me.

"Jase used to hold my hand when I was scared," I say, wincing as the pilot slams the cabin door shut.

I look down at my empty palm.

"He doesn't hold my hand anymore."

Elliot crosses his ankles, pursing his lips as he grabs my hand. "You know what your problem is, Julz?"

"I've got ninety-nine problems, El. Narrow it down for me."

"Your problem is, you stopped being angry. You stopped being vengeful. Where's that furious girl who killed all the people who did her wrong? Where's that girl who danced in the dark?"

Ow. I shrug. "She's dead."

Elliot shakes his head. "No, she's not." He taps my forehead with his index finger. "She's in here. And you've got about five hours to find her and drag her sorry ass back out here."

CHAPTER TWELVE

Juliette

I'm anxious as hell, but I must be exhausted, too. Everyone picks a seat, the plane takes off, and as soon as we're clear of the weather I fall asleep. I might hate flying, but the one very reassuring thing about it is, nobody can really get to us up here. It's like we're suspended from reality for a few short hours, and unless someone is good enough to shoot the plane down, we're golden. I don't think that'd ever happen. The Gypsies and the Cartel are full of the kind of men who want to watch you die on your knees in front of them, not shoot you out of the sky.

We get to LA, land at a private airstrip, and what a greeting we receive.

We land beside a square car full of LAPD officers, and the sight both worries and relieves me. Elliot's called in a favor at the last minute, and it seems the guys from his old precinct—not to mention his female Captain—are on hand to make sure nothing befalls us. We split up, Elliot riding with Amy and Kayla in his Captain's car, and Jase and I riding with Luis and a couple of LAPD officers Elliot has worked with before. The Los Angeles PD couldn't help us with our DEA dramas since it's a federal case we're part of, so I'm very grateful that they've bent the rules to escort us safely for the final part of our journey back to ground zero. From what Elliot said, they're helping us on their time, and if anyone finds out, they could lose their jobs.

Before I know it we're rolling down the I-5, the sky blue and wide here. It's a welcome relief, in an odd way. The Cartel is closing in. We're in the stronghold of the Gypsy Brothers, the city of Los Angeles. And yet ... I know this place. It's in my bones. It's the place I was born, the place I grew up. For better or for worse: It's my home.

The humidity is gone, replaced with a dry, gentle heat that makes my brain fog lift considerably. I can actually think straight for the first time in forever.

A couple hours later, we're showered, dressed and sitting around a large round table in the middle of the large, nondescript safe house we've been installed into in Hollywood. It's got ten bedrooms, ten bathrooms, an indoor waterfall and an infinity pool that hugs a steep hillside overlooking the city. So much for being discreet.

"Where'd you find this place?" I ask Luis as we wait for Elliot to arrive.

"Airbnb," Luis replies, winking. Funny thing is, he's probably telling the truth. I raise my eyebrows, running my hand over the smooth wooden dining table and praying we aren't tracked to this place. I'd hate this beautiful gangster mansion to get shot up just because we're here.

Once Elliot's arrived, there's a collective silence for a few moments. I already feel a little better just being on home turf. I know these streets like the back of my hand, and I know all the favorite Gypsy haunts. I feel like I could see danger a lot easier here than I could in Miami. And, finally, it feels like something is about to happen. I'm tired of living in limbo. Tired of running.

And judging by the faces around me, I'm not the only one. Jase sits to my right, Elliot to my left, and Tommy and Luis are across from me. Everyone's on edge, but everyone's handling their shit. There's a thread of controlled excitement binding the five of us together at this table, and we haven't even started to talk.

And I have a feeling it's because we've finally gotten sick of hiding, of running, and following orders and waiting around. For once, we've made our own decision. We're not going to follow orders anymore. We're going to fight this war, on our own terms. And we've brought the fight back home.

"So," Elliot says, lounging back in his chair like we aren't all being chased by an international drug syndicate and a lethal biker gang. "Who wants the table? Julz? How's that vengeance going?"

I roll my eyes. "It's on a low simmer."

"Well, crank that shit up to eleven. We don't want crying Julz. We want crazy Julz."

I smile thinly. "I'll work on my personal development between now and tonight," I quip.

"Tommy? How's that DEA intel coming along?"

Tommy licks his lips, shrugging. "I don't have any hard evidence, but I'm pretty convinced that Fitzsimmons was the one who gave your location away in Miami. Which is why he doesn't know I'm here."

Elliot nods. "Luis," he says. "Bring any fun toys in your jet for us?"

Luis smiles wickedly. "Maybe I got a rocket launcher and twenty-four IEDs. Maybe I don't."

Elliot narrows his eyes. "If you have a rocket launcher, I want to use it."

Luis slaps the table with his open palm. "The rocket launcher is mine. I've got AKs for you civilians."

"Who you calling a civilian?" Elliot asks.

"You *are* a civilian," Tommy pipes up. "I, on the other hand, should be allowed to be in charge of the rocket launcher."

"Maybe we should figure out what the fuck we're going to do in the next hour and forty-five minutes," Jase interjects. He's the least congenial of all of us, and I can't blame him. He's deeply worried. I can see the cracks starting to appear. He's tired, he's jumpy, and he's pissed the fuck off.

"We hit them where it hurts," I say. Four pairs of eyes turn to me. "The clubhouse. Tomorrow. It's Sunday tomorrow. They'll all be there for church."

Jase looks apprehensive. "We don't have any weapons here."

Luis pokes his thumb towards the front of the house. "They're in the garage," he says.

"Oh," Jase says. "Well."

"Remind me again why we're meeting this FBI agent at a sex club?" Tommy asks. "Like, why do we need her?"

Jase rolls his eyes. "Because she can get us off."

Luis grins, Tommy laughs, Elliot sucks his cheeks in to stop himself from losing it, and Jase looks at the ceiling. Even I'm struggling not to laugh.

"Oh, Jase," I say, squeezing his shoulder. "You walked right into that one."

He shakes his head, trying to compose himself. "Because she's offered to talk to her boss and see if the FBI can't do something for us."

"Why didn't you call her earlier?" Elliot asks. "Couldn't she have helped us six months ago?"

"She was undercover," Jase says. "I didn't know where she was. She's been back in the field office for a few weeks. Used to be DEA. As soon as I told her about Fitz she started telling me about his dirty operations."

Jealousy stirs in my stomach. She must have called him for him to know this.

"She told you Fitz was dirty weeks ago?" I ask. "And you didn't say anything?"

"She said she had a hunch," Jase replies. "She didn't have any evidence. But DEA agents don't wear Rolex watches and drive Beamers unless they've got rich families. And this guy's family is broke as fuck. So someone must be paying him off. Isobel thinks it's the Cartel paying him money to work both sides of the line."

"They have hot bitches at this sex club?" Luis asks.

Elliot looks offended. "Don't call them bitches," he says, nodding his head towards me.

"Why?" I shrug. "I want to know if they have hot bitches, too."

Tommy looks confused. "Why are we meeting at a sex club, anyway? Won't they notice us fully clothed and packing heat?"

Jase looks exasperated. "Look," he says. "The whole point of this place is security. No weapons in. No wires. For anyone. You check your guns at the door, and you get scanned. So it's the safest place. At least, the safest place for an FBI agent who's meeting four of America's most wanted fugitives."

Tommy clears his throat.

"And one badass biker from Venice Beach," Jase adds. Tommy smiles, but the gesture doesn't reach his eyes. He looks pained.

"How you want to handle your dad, man?" Jase asks Tommy quietly.

"I'm getting him out," Tommy says. "I know what you're all

thinking, but he's not like the rest of them. He's not."

Viper is one of the most notorious Gypsy Brothers, but I have to agree with Tommy. He's not the same as Dornan and his sons were. There are men with questionable morals and then there are men like Dornan Ross.

"He knows I'm DEA," Tommy blurts out. "He's known for years."

Jase's eyebrows almost hit the roof. "Seriously? How do we know he's not gonna stab us in the back?"

"Because he's already gone," Tommy grinds out.

Jase sits back in his seat. "Are you fucking kidding me, Tommy?"

"No kidding, brother."

"You told your dad you were DEA, and you didn't tell me?" Jase asks him. "I thought you trusted me, Tommy. You're like my brother."

"I trust you now," Tommy replies. This is the first time I've seen Tommy get into a heated discussion. "I didn't trust you when you came back from lockdown, Jason. You were a fucking psycho, and you know it. If Julz hadn't turned up, who knows what you'd be doing now."

"Enough," Jase says. "Viper gets a pass. If I ever find him doing anything that could threaten us, I'm putting *him* to ground myself."

Tommy nods his head in agreement.

"You ever shot a machine gun, pretty lady?" Luis asks me.

I snort. "Please. I lived with Elliot for three years. I can shoot better than he can."

"Well, all right then," Luis says. He pushes a piece of paper into the middle of the table and we all lean in on our elbows for a better look.

It's building plans for the Gypsy Brothers clubhouse. A thrill shoots through me as I listen to Luis detail all of the entries and exits, the fire escapes and basement hatches, and Tommy leans in to highlight the best places to pack explosives.

It's happened so quickly, it's almost like it isn't happening. This morning, hours ago, I was crying into a comforter, wondering if I was going to get ambushed and shot if I dared take a shower. And now, I'm back in LA—we all are, this band of misfits with a common cause: to take down the Gypsy Brothers MC and the Il Sangue Cartel, once and for all.

CHAPTER THIRTEEN

Jase

I remember the day Dornan Ross locked me up and left me to rot.

He'd just returned from taking Juliette to the hospital. *She's alive, she's alive,* that's what I kept telling myself. *Pop won't let her die. He can't. She knows where the money is.* Even I didn't know where Juliette's father had hidden the money Mariana had siphoned from the Cartel's bank accounts over a period of almost ten years.

I remember the way the gun felt too heavy in my hand, loaded with a single bullet. My dad, fucking psychopath that he was, had already shot John Portland for sleeping with his woman. He shot him in the dick. I can still hear him groaning, the way his blood soaked the ground around him.

What a way to die. I can't imagine anywhere worse to bleed out, as a guy. It was a deliberate choice of shot for my dad—fuck Dornan's woman and it's the last woman you'll ever stick your cock inside.

I still think about it sometimes, when I look at Juliette and see her father's face. It's harder to see now, with the way she changed her cheekbones and her nose to slip under Dornan's radar when she blew back into town, looking for vengeance. But I can see him there. I still look at the woman I love and am haunted by the fact that I killed her father. I mean, he was going to die anyway, but it still makes me hate myself that it was me who planted a bullet in his brain.

I don't know why I'm thinking about this now. Maybe it's because I'm watching Juliette as she looks out of our bedroom window and realize that she and her father have—*had*—the exact same shaped skull.

Maybe I'm just feeling guilty today.

"I never thought I'd be happy to be back in Los Angeles," she says, staring out of the window to the Hollywood sign in the hills.

"Come away from there," I say, tugging her hand. "Your hair's like this big homing beacon." I smile as I say it, ruffling her long red strands with my fingers.

"I don't want you to come to this meeting," I say. "No lies. I'm being honest. I don't know which of these fucking people we can trust, Julz, and I don't want you caught in the crossfire. I want you to be safe."

She puts her hand on my cheek, stepping forward so I have to take a step back. She pushes me until I'm backed up against the bed, pressing my shoulders so I sit down on the edge.

"And I'm coming to the meeting anyway," she says, smiling sweetly as she straddles me. I'm hard almost instantly; I don't know if it's our impending doom or the way her t-shirt hugs her tits, but I want to fuck her more than I have in a long time.

Maybe it's because there's an awesome chance that we're both going to die tonight.

I bite her nipple through the thin t-shirt material and hear her gasp. That's enough for me. I grab her and set her on her feet in front of me, ripping her jeans and panties down to her ankles. Smiling, she kicks them off, getting back into my lap. I unzip my pants and palm my cock, precum already leaking all over the tip. There's no time for foreplay. No time for getting my tongue onto her clit and making her nice and soaked before I slam balls-deep into her tight cunt. There's just no time.

Greedily, I pull her hips closer with one hand, lining my cock up with her pussy with the other. "Sit," I demand, and she does, crying out loudly as she takes all of me in one go. Her eyes go wide as I fill her up, and it takes every single bit of self-control I possess to stop myself from flipping her over and pounding her into the mattress until she screams.

And now she's in my lap, my hands itching to leave bruises all over her pale flesh. Her pussy squeezes my cock so tight it hurts, and just when I think I'm going to come, she slows down. She stops.

"What's wrong?" I ask, my cock impatient, my mind very much aware that we've got about three minutes before we have to leave for the meeting at The Black Heart.

"Nothing," Julz pants, kissing me with a hunger that makes me want to fuck her so hard she screams. It's good that she's on top of me, because if she was underneath me, I doubt I'd be able to restrain myself from pounding her pussy until she begged me to stop.

"What's The Black Heart?" Julz whispers, planting kisses down my neck. Sucking. *Oh.* She's leaving her mark. Something about the way she's making sure she's imprinted on my skin makes me almost unload in her right this second. My cock twitches, but I grit my teeth and breathe, breathe it out, calm the fuck down.

"Can we talk about this later?" I grind out, lifting her hips and letting her fall. She locks her knees around my hips so I can't maneuver her anymore, squeezing her pussy walls tighter around my dick.

"Jesus," I say. "Keep doing that and I'll be coming inside you right now."

She smiles, bringing her mouth to mine, kissing me like she's about to fucking eat me. I let my hands go to her tits, pinching her nipples so she gasps.

"Something happened to you," she says breathlessly between kisses, "and you're going to tell me. Maybe not today. Maybe not for a long time. But, Jason, you're going to tell me." And I can't argue, because she starts bouncing on my cock again and I can't say any words, especially not harsh ones. Goddamn her. It's an excellent strategy, as far as strategies go.

I swallow thickly, groaning as Julz picks up her pace. All I can do is sit back, my fingers around her hips, as she sets the pace. As she controls this. Of course, I could flip her over with my little finger, but I can tell she's getting off on this, more than she's gotten off in a long time. Maybe the threat of us dying tonight is enough for her to focus on having one last mind-blowing fuck.

"What happened at The Black Heart?" Julz asks again, and this time I do stop her. I flip her over, so I'm on top of her, my cock as deep as possible as I place a hand on each of her knees and start thrusting.

"Oh, FUCK," she yells, loud enough for the entire place to hear as she fists the sheets on either side of her. I slap a hand over her mouth to shut her up. Her eyes fly open as her pussy tightens around me and her eyes roll back in her head. She comes as soon as my palm tightens around her face, her hips lifting up from the bed as her whole body locks, and the way she's wrapped around my cock sends me over the edge. I come inside her, shuddering as wave after wave milks my cock of everything it's got.

CHAPTER FOURTEEN

Juliette

Isobel Sazerac is beautiful. I hate her immediately.

She's got chocolate-brown hair that falls in loose waves around her face, stopping at her shoulders, and high cheekbones with skin the consistency of a dewy peach. She wears lashings of dark eyeliner that makes her blue eyes pop—real blue eyes, as far as I can tell—and has long fingers that look like they should be playing piano, not scrawling case notes and shooting target practice at the range. Or whatever the fuck it is FBI agents do.

Maybe it's because I take one look at the way she greets Jase and I know they've screwed before. Probably in this club. Maybe because she's hot as fuck, dressed in matching black silk bra and panties and standing in front of the three of us, her hands on her hips. Elliot and Tommy are on watch outside the club, which leaves me standing between Jase and Luis.

"Strip," she says, and I'm suddenly reminded of a scene just like this, when we had to strip in front of Pepito and the Skullz Cartel members to prove we weren't wearing wires.

"Seriously?" I ask. "Your bodyguard just scanned us with that thing and took all our weapons. We're not wearing wires."

She shrugs, apparently not perturbed by me in the slightest. "I don't make the rules," she replies. "You don't have to strip, but if you don't, they won't let us past the cloak room."

On either side of me, Jase and Luis are undressing. Rolling my eyes, I do the same, folding my jeans and black t-shirt in a neat pile at my feet. I leave my boots on. I might need to kick somebody's face in if they try to rub against me in there. I'm suddenly acutely aware of the scar tissue that trails from underneath my breasts all the way down my side and over my hip bone. There used to be seven horizontal scars there, then a beautiful tattoo that Elliot inked to cover up said scars. Now, there's just marred, uneven flesh that looks like it's been melted off with a blowtorch. *Thanks, Dornan.*

"What about your tattoos?' I say, turning to press my fingers against Jase's massive Gypsy Brothers brand that adorns his back. Luis has one too. We'll be spotted in no time. Two rogue Gypsy Brothers hanging about, mere miles from the clubhouse where bikers are assembling, hungry for our blood. Great.

The bodyguard next to Isobel steps forward with a stack of black material in his hands. As he hands one of the pieces to each of us, I see that they're black satin robes. Thank Christ for that.

Five minutes later, Luis and I are standing in the corner of a large room that reminds me very much of an upmarket strip club, with a lot more fucking. There are people fucking on a pool table while a small crowd gathers around them and watches. There's a woman leaning against a stripper pole on an elevated stage with another woman's head between her thighs, and a guy taking that girl from behind. Further up, there's a blindfolded guy getting face-fucked by a line of waiting erections of varying shapes and sizes. As I'm looking around the room, I'm not sure if I'm kind of aroused or completely confused about what's going on in here. I've never been much of a voyeur, but some of the people here are extremely attractive.

I'm so preoccupied by what's happening in the distance that I don't see the dick in my face until it's almost too late. Well, it's not really in my face—more like at my stomach height—but this one-eyed monster is pointed right at me. Which is very unsettling. It's attached to a large, very nicely built guy with shaggy blond hair and dimples.

"You're beautiful," he says, admiring me openly. I haven't bothered to knot my robe in the front since everyone else here is completely naked, so my underwear is visible in the slit the gown makes down my middle.

"Are you a natural redhead?" He stares pointedly at my panties.

"Not even slightly," I say, flashing him a mouth full of teeth. I grab Luis's hand, turning so I'm facing him and away from monster cock. "Help me," I say through my teeth, smiling and raising my eyebrows at him. Luis tries his hardest not to crack a smile, pulling me towards him until my head rests against his shoulder. I stay there for a moment, waiting until the guy's gone, and then Luis pushes me gently. I straighten my hair and decide now's a great time to knot my gown shut. "What do you think he wanted?" I whisper, watching as monster cock finds a willing victim. I tilt my head, blinking in disbelief as someone actually attempts to suck that thing into their mouth.

"I think he wanted to take you to the candy shop," Luis says, and I can tell he's trying so hard not to laugh. "Let you lick the lollipop."

I elbow Luis, refocusing my attention on the door where Jase and Isobel disappeared. I'm not worried about Jase cheating on me, but I am worried about Isobel still having the hots for him. She looks like she knows a good thing when she sees it. And Jase is definitely a good-looking thing.

"Five more minutes," I say to Luis. "Five more, and I'm going back there to find them."

Luis nods. Sometimes I think he'd do anything I say. I wonder why. I've done nothing for him during the time we've know each other except be a needy pain in the ass. I think he's sentimental, or something. I think he knows how much his mama loved Jase and I. He wants to be a part of the action, and so far he's been front and center.

"You think this is going to work tonight?" I ask Luis.

He shrugs. "I certainly fucking hope so, bebé."

I square my shoulders. "I'm tired of waiting. I'm going in. Wait for me?"

Luis shrugs in agreement and watches me as I go searching for Jase and his pretty FBI pal.

CHAPTER FIFTEEN

Jase

I'd been out of the cell, that dank fuckhole my father kept me in, for a couple months, and my crazy was just getting started. I was on fire with rage and sex feeding my every move. I was banned from Va Va Voom, the strip club run by the Gypsies, after I almost killed a girl while I was fucking her. In the ass. In a booth. While I wrapped her stockings around her neck and pulled until she turned blue underneath me.

So what does a sex-crazed, psychotic guy do when he's been denied the free pussy he's always been able to access?

He finds more pussy. Better pussy. Pussy that likes to be choked, even if you have to pay handsomely for the privilege of a little violence.

I ended up stumbling upon The Black Heart by chance, after the DEA agent whose number I'd memorized agreed to meet with me. Amanda Hoyne. I still remember the hours I'd spent in the dark, in the hole, reciting the number John had given me before I shot him dead. Amanda Hoyne. She was the one I could trust.

So I met Amanda Hoyne, and it turns out I was way above her fucking pay grade. It was her, ironically, who directed me to the club and to her DEA superior. She met me in a bar in West Hollywood, took one look at me and handed me a matte black business card with an address printed on the back and a picture of an anatomical black heart, arteries and all, the edges embossed and raised slightly from the rest of the card. The first chance I got, I went to that club, and in hindsight they were obviously expecting me, because I didn't need a password, or ID, or even a smile. I just asked for Isobel Sazerac and waltzed in like I owned the place. I didn't know back then if she was somebody I could trust, but my curiosity about The Black Heart and my raging desire to fuck somebody in the dark until they passed out won out over everything else.

They let me in, and next thing I knew I had my pants around my ankles and my hands around the throat of the prettiest little submissive I'd ever seen, while she swallowed my cock. There was no chase. No force. No dubious consent. The women (and men) who visited The Black Heart were there because they were as devious and as disturbed as me. The tighter I squeezed, the faster they climaxed. The harder I fucked them, the more they asked me to do it again. There was no shame. No bullets.

No Dornan, unless you counted me, and the way I was starting to become him.

I'd been going to The Black Heart for a couple months, just a few times a week to keep my demons at bay while I figured out what the hell my next move against my father would be, when I finally did the deed with Isobel. Before then, we'd talk, and she'd promise me all kinds of things that sounded interesting and dubious, like avenging Juliette's death and making my father and brothers pay for their sins. She was talking jail time. I figured that was a good starting point. Once I contained them, then I could work on extinguishing them. Once we screwed the first time, it was like a race to see who could be the kinkiest, the most perverted. She had a particular fondness for sex swings and blindfolds, now that I remember.

So to be here, back in this club, is the weirdest fucking experience. I'm trying so, so hard to focus on what Isobel's telling me about the DEA's shady operations and how Fitz is likely using us as bait that he'll then trade off to the Cartel, and I'm getting about ninety percent of what she's saying, but the other ten percent is getting lost as I watch the scene unfolding over her shoulder.

See, the front room of The Black Heart is for fucking and dancing and drinking. Plain and simple. But the back area—walled off and behind a wall of extra security—is the place where you can indulge almost any desire.

And right behind Isobel, I'm watching two guys dominate a girl who looks very similar to Juliette. Not as pretty, but superficially similar. Long legs, hips and ass to hold onto, a generous rack that long brown strands cascade down onto. She's being fucked in the front and the back, and the guys are taking turns choking her with a silk tie.

"You want to swap seats?" Isobel asks, craning her neck over her shoulder.

I shake my head, shifting to try and stop my raging hard-on from breaking through my boxers and into the night.

"You know, this is the first time we've met here and not touched each other," she says, grinning wryly. "To think how far we've come."

I snort. "You mean you're not still roaming the halls of The Black Heart, waiting for me to come back?"

"Ha," she says, finishing the drink she's been cradling for our entire conversation. "They have sex clubs in San Francisco, Jason. They have men there, too. Good-looking ones."

"I bet they do," I reply.

"We done here?"

I nod. "Thank you for coming."

"Thank you for coming," she mimics me, scowling for good measure. Then the scowl morphs into a smile as she reaches her stiletto out and kicks my shin. "I missed you," she says. "I'm glad you found her again. What was it like when you realized it was her?"

I smile faintly, remembering the moment I stopped seeing Sammi and started seeing Juliette under the plastic surgery and the tattoo and the hair dye. It was almost instant. Once I'd seen her again as Juliette, it could never be unseen.

"It was like waking up from the worst nightmare you've ever had," I murmur.

She seems to like it when I say that. Of course she would. She's one of the people who saw all the worst parts of my soul.

"I have to go," Isobel says, standing. "Call me after whatever goes down, goes down. I know nothing. We never spoke. Yeah?"

"Yeah."

"Give me a head start before you leave. If anyone sees us leaving together who knows anything, we're both fucked."

"Got it."

Isobel leaves, patting my shoulder as she departs. And in my rational brain, I know I should follow her. I know I should get out of this room and at least hang with Luis and Julz for five minutes until Isobel's had a chance to get away from the place.

But the scene unfolding in front of me is so fucking mesmerizing, I can't move.

The two guys are being rough with the girl who's sandwiched between them. Like, really rough. One of them is biting every inch of her exposed skin, the other choking her until she sags between them and then slapping her until she comes to. He slaps her really hard, and my cock jumps in my boxers.

Jesus, fuck, I have to get out of here.

I can't move.

My hands are shaking.

My hands are shaking and my mouth is dry. I want to do what they're doing. I want to go over and wrap my hands around that girl's neck and squeeze until she passes out.

"Jase," a voice says beside me, and I just about jump out of my fucking seat.

It's Julz. Her eyes are as round as dinner plates as she watches what I'm watching. I thought she'd turn away in disgust or demand that we leave, but she's just as captivated as me.

"That looks hot," she says, and I can hardly believe my ears.

"Huh?"

"It's hot. What they're doing. Don't you think?" Her last sentence is tinged with uncertainty, like I've just caught her doing something she's not supposed to be doing.

I break my focus on the threesome in front of us to study Juliette. I stand, moving behind her, pressing my rock-hard cock into her back as she stands straighter.

"You like the look of that?" I whisper in her ear. "Which part?"

She swallows hard, her breathing speeding up. "The biting," she says quietly. "The silk tie. The—violence in their touch."

I take a deep breath. Fuck it. My meeting with Isobel was quick, and there's a very good chance we might be dead by tomorrow.

"Anything about what they're doing that you don't like?"

She shakes her head. "Nope."

Growling under my breath, I take Juliette's upper arm and start half-walking, half-dragging her deeper into the labyrinth of private rooms that people pay thousands of dollars to hire out by the hour: safe spaces to explore their wildest fantasies, their most taboo desires. I try the first handle, but it's locked. The second gives, and I push it open with lightning speed, hauling Juliette into the room and locking the door behind her.

I don't even stop to see what kind of furniture the room consists of. I throw Juliette on the floor and pounce on her like I'm a lion and she's my catch.

My dick's inside her within three seconds of the door closing, even though it's dark in here, the only light from a couple of candles throwing off weak light. It could be the middle of the day and I wouldn't have a clue, because all I can see is Juliette Portland underneath me, her legs spread and her pussy full of me. I put my hands around her neck. I want to squeeze. I want to choke her so fucking badly. *Goddamn it!* I stop grinding my cock into her. I just *stop*.

"I don't want to hurt you," I whisper in the dark. "Julz, the things I used to do in this place—I used to hurt people and get off on it. I don't want to hurt you, baby."

She reaches up and grabs hold of my face; I can just make out her eyes, her pupils almost swallowing any trace of green.

"Jase," she breathes. "*What if I want you to hurt me*?"

I'm dubious. There's hurting and there's hurting. She feels my uncertainty; she must.

"Fuck me," she says. "Bite me. Make me bleed. Choke me. I'm yours. I trust you."

And goddamn if that isn't the hottest thing I've heard in my entire existence.

I do what she says. I fuck her. I bite her. And then I take her back to the place we're staying and I do it again. I fuck her. I choke her. I love her in the only way I know how.

CHAPTER SIXTEEN

Juliette

My phone vibrates on the nightstand. I think about ignoring it, but I can't. Not when it could be something important. Something life and death.

Then again, what isn't life and death in our existence?

I grab at the phone and turn it over in my hand, squinting at the screen. My heart leaps into my mouth when I see Agent Dunn's cell number come up. She's using her burner phone to call mine. I haven't spoken to her in months, not since we were in Colorado and she tipped me off about the Cartel closing ranks on us. That was the first time we'd had to run, but it wasn't the last.

I press the green button and bring the phone to my ear, almost in slow motion.

"Hello?" I hear a voice down the other end. It's Agent Dunn. Though she's technically with the CIA, and the CIA controls the Gypsy Brothers MC and the Il Sangue Cartel, she's more trustworthy than most, but that doesn't exactly mean a lot to me right now.

"Yes?" I say, my voice hoarse. I watch the steady rise and fall of Jase's chest as he sleeps beside me. It's the first time he's slept soundly beside me in a very long time. I guess he needs a rest after all of the things we just did. Honestly, my mind is still reeling from the violent fucking I've just been given; I'm so sore I doubt I'll be walking properly in the morning, and my chest and thighs are covered in hickeys and bite marks. My scalp is sore and tingling from where Jase pulled my hair.

It was, hands down, the best sex I've ever had in my life.

I can't think about that now, though. I've got to talk to Agent Dunn.

"What's going on," I ask. "Everything okay?"

"Are you with Jason Ross?" she asks, her tone scaring me.

"I'm alone," I say, padding into the bathroom that adjoins our temporary room and closing the door. I close the toilet lid and sit on it, draping a towel over my legs to stave off the cold morning air. The sun's just starting to peek over the horizon, and I'm annoyed she's called so early.

Still. Must be urgent. Sounds urgent.

"If anyone finds out I called you, I'll lose my kid and my job," she says.

"Okay," I say. "You know you can trust me. At least, I hope you do." And it's true, she can trust me. After what went down in Furnace Creek, I developed a newfound respect for Agent Dunn. She might have started off as a pain in my ass, but she became useful in the end. And the fact she tipped us off about the Cartel and the CIA coming for us in Colorado—well, I trust her.

"What's going on? How bad is it?"

She's quiet. Now I'm really worried.

"You know we found several bodies buried on Emilio Ross's estate in San Diego, yes?"

"Yeah," I say, my mouth suddenly very dry. "I saw it on the news."

"Juliette, I don't even know if I should be telling you this, but we've done DNA testing on them, finally, and we found something."

"Is the punchline coming soon?" I ask. "What'd you find?"

I can hear her hesitation. "The bodies were female, between the ages of fifteen and twenty-six. They found DNA inside the women. Semen. These women had been raped and killed."

"Jesus," I say. "Dornan's DNA?"

"No," Agent Dunn breathes. "Not Dornan's. Jason's."

I stand up and push the bathroom door open to see the man I love is awake and staring straight back at me from the edge of our bed. The bed still marked with our blood from the love bites we gave each other just hours ago.

Oh, God.

"You're positive?" I ask her, as I hold Jase's gaze.

"It was a clean match," she says. This can't be happening. This cannot be happening.

"How many?" I ask her. I'm not sure if I want to know.

She tells me. And I wish she hadn't.

"Thank you," I say. "I have to go."

I don't wait for her to answer; I end the call, still not taking my eyes from Jase.

"I'm done waiting," I say to him, my voice too calm, my hands too steady.

"You tell me what happened in that place you call the hole. You tell me, or so help me God, I will never speak to you again."

Jase's eyes narrow. He stands and comes towards me; I step back. "Don't touch me," I say. "Just start talking."

"Sure, I'll talk," he says. "On one condition."

CHAPTER SEVENTEEN

Juliette

"You answer one question," Jase says to me, "and I'll tell you everything that happened while you were gone and I was underground for three fucking years. One question."

"Ask me," I reply. "Ask me. I'll tell you anything."

"Where do you go?" he asks slowly, his eyes boring into me.

I expected it to be something entirely different. Something about the drugs or the pregnancy or fucking Dornan. Anything.

"What do you mean? Where do I go *when*?"

His fingers tighten at his sides, forming fists.

"When you blank out. When you go away. You're with him, aren't you?"

I take a step back. I feel like I've been punched. I don't respond. I don't even say *who do you mean*, because we both know who we're talking about here.

"Hey," Jase snaps. "I want you to answer me."

I can't breathe. It's like Dornan's in the room. I feel his warm breath on my neck, the way he always tasted the same in my mouth. Like salt and cigarettes.

"Answer me," Jase growls.

I break. "What?" I hiss. "What do you want from me? Do you want me to lie? I was supposed to kill him, and that was meant to be the end of it."

Jase looks like he's about to hit another wall. Or me.

"He's dead," he spits. "He's dead, but *you're* the one who's gone. I need you to come back. I need you to come back to me."

"I don't know how!" I yell.

"You're not trying!" he explodes. "You just sit here, in your dark little universe, thinking about him! Did you think about him while I was fucking you last night? Huh?"

I don't even know where this is coming from. I thought after what we'd just done in that bedroom, that things might get better.

"I try," I reply. "I try! Every time I fucking try you're here, and you look—" Oh, fuck. This is going somewhere very, very bad. I cover my face with my hands. I don't want to cry. I'm so fucking tired of crying. *Emilio's compound. Jase's DNA.* I think I'm going to throw up.

Through my splayed fingers, I see Jase rub his chin, visibly agitated. "I look just like him. Right?"

Right.

"I didn't say that," I whisper. *Just like him.*

"Oh, yes, you did. That's exactly what you were going to say. What is it, huh? My eyes? You want me to burn my fucking eyes out? What else, huh? WHAT ELSE?" Jase is angry. He's so, so angry.

And I don't know what to do to fix it this time.

"Please, just stop." I'm begging.

"So you can't talk to me. You can't look at me. But you can fuck me. You don't mind me tying you to a bed and fucking you, and hurting you, but you can't tell me the truth. Right? What is this? Please, fucking please, just help me to understand."

"I loved him!" I cry. "I loved him! He was like my father, before I even knew my father. He was my protector. He was the one I went to when I had a problem and I didn't want my parents to know. And he always loved me back. He always fixed things. My own mother didn't know what to do with me, and he was always there and *I loved him.*"

Jase growls, picking up the water glass beside him and throwing it as hard as he can at the wall. It shatters, bits of plaster and porcelain flying everywhere. I take a deep breath. "You want me to stop?"

He glares at me. "No."

"He just … it was like he changed, from one hour to the next. He was someone who loved me, and then he wasn't. And I miss him. Not the person who did all those things to me. I miss the man who brought me home from the hospital. I miss the man who protected me. I miss knowing who I am, where my place is in the world. I'm not anybody. I don't have a name. I don't have a home. I don't have anything. I wish I could take those bullets back, because I don't want him dead. I want him here, so I can ask him why."

"You know why," Jase says. "You know why he did that. He did that to ruin your father, because some fucking woman chose your father over him, and he couldn't live with that. So he took you, and he turned you into a sacrificial vessel for everything anyone had ever done wrong by him. Everything. And afterwards, when he thought you were dead, he realized what a colossal fucking mistake he'd made. He wished he could take it back, okay?" Jase's eyes are wild. "He told me he was sorry for what he did. He told me he wished he could take it back. And I believed him. Is that what you wanted to hear?"

Jase is covering his face with his hands now. He's shaking his head, and then he looks up again at me, his eyes so fucking sad, but more worrying than that, they're resigned.

"You promised you'd tell me," I say.

He looks up at the ceiling.

"Nothing you did will change the way I feel about you!" I say. "But if you don't tell me, I don't know how to deal with this. I don't know how to trust you if you can't trust me with this. What did you do?"

He looks back at me and his eyes are red and glossy, his jaw set. He grabs my wrists, squeezing so hard it hurts, but I'm not afraid.

"I love you," he says, his voice thick with emotion. "I love you and I want you to know that, because you're going to hate me in a moment."

"Jason."

He takes a deep breath and closes his eyes. "I killed your father."

"I know that. It was a mercy killing. I forgive you."

His hands continue to squeeze my wrists. He's so close I can see the wet spots in the corners of his eyes, where the tears want to spill out. He won't open his eyes. Won't look at me.

"After I killed him, after they told me you were dead, they gave me something to make me sleep. Everything was dark, and cold, and I didn't understand. I thought that maybe I was dead, too. But I wasn't. I was alive, I was very much alive. When I woke up it was still dark. It was always dark."

He's whispering all of this. He hasn't opened his eyes, and he hasn't let go of my wrists. He leans his head forward, his forehead touching against mine.

"My father and Chad tied me to a chair and put a sock in my mouth. I fought them, Juliette, I fought so hard, but there were always too many of them. It was never a fair fight."

My chest constricts as I remember being held down by them. He's right. There were always more of them. It was never a fair fight. His fingers keep squeezing my wrists so hard, I can't feel my hands anymore.

"My father brought a girl into my dark little room and made her … *suck me* while he held a gun to her head. She was scared. We were both so scared. I tried to scream but the sock—I couldn't make her stop. I couldn't make him stop."

He tied me to a chair, too. I wasn't really his daughter, but Jase was really his son.

"I didn't finish. I didn't even get hard. I couldn't have, even if I'd wanted to. Because all I could see was you and what they did to you. He made me keep my eyes open. He said he'd shoot her if I didn't watch the screen."

The screen?

"I watched it every day, every single day. The tape went for two hours. One hundred and twenty minutes before it cut out. It always cut out when you were crying. When you were begging me to help you."

I choke on a sob as what he's telling me sinks in. Oh God. Oh God. It wasn't enough that Dornan recorded them raping me. He made Jase watch it every day for three years.

"I did what he said. I turned into a monster. I hurt those girls, a different one every day. I fucked them and I bit them and I made *them* bleed. As long as I did what he said, he let them go. He killed the first girl, and Chad killed the last. Did they find both of their bodies?"

I sigh, the weight of reality almost too much to bear.

"Not two bodies," I whisper. "They found more than two bodies."

Jase's eyes fly open. I can see all the blood vessels in the whites of his eyes as he pulls his head away from mine. They're angry eyes. Even the tiny veins in his beautiful eyes are full of the rage and grief he carries inside him like a cancer.

"*What*?"

I can't tell him. I have to tell him.

"Jason," I say softly. "He didn't let them go. They've found sixteen girls buried in your grandfather's compound so far. He didn't let any of them go."

CHAPTER EIGHTEEN

Jase

There's an angry buzz in my head. It's getting louder, and more painful, like someone's drilling into my skull. I can't hear anything except the words Juliette's just spoken to me.

Sixteen

Six-fucking-teen!

She's talking, but I can't hear her. The words are all garbled.

I get up. I lock myself in the bathroom as my vision clouds red.

I lean on the basin and stare at myself in the large mirror.

Sixteen.

I try to remember their faces. Some are there, in my memory. Some I didn't even get to see—I just felt them underneath me as I hurt them in the dark.

I think how the last thing they saw before they died was me.

I'm a monster.

Of course I look just like Dornan.

I've become him.

I make my hand into a fist and smash it into my reflection. The glass splinters, but it doesn't break. So I do it again. And again. It must be tempered glass, because the cracks I'm smashing into it don't spread and splinter.

I do it again. And again. My fist is a mess of blood, running down my arm and splattering on my face, but I don't stop. I don't ever want to see that face again.

The violence soothes me. With every punch, there's more blood, and my hearing starts to return in waves.

Juliette's on the other side of the door. She's screaming at me to open up, and she's kicking the door.

My girl just found out the worst, most depraved things I've ever done, and instead of running away, she's kicking the goddamn door down to try and get to me.

"Jason!" She screams. "Open this door right fucking now or I'm shooting it open!"

I stop pummeling the glass. I look at the door in disbelief.

"You're not going to shoot the door open to get in here," I call out to her, panting after the sudden exertion. "I'm no good for you, Julz. You deserve better. Just go. Just walk away from me."

"Get away from the door, Jase," she yells.

And she shoots the goddamn lock out of the door.

"Fuck!" I yell, as she kicks the door open and drops her gun onto the tiled floor. She flies at me, launching into my arms as she wraps her legs around my hips and her arms around my neck.

She's crying as she kisses me. She's getting my blood on her.

"You stupid man," she says, breaking the kiss long enough to rear back and slap me across the face. Then she kisses me again, her salty tears running into my mouth.

"Julz," I protest, turning my head to the side to break the kiss.

"Don't you dare tell me to walk away," she says, grabbing my face in her hands and forcing me to look at her. Her green eyes are blazing.

"Don't you dare tell me I deserve better. I deserve to be happy, and you make me happy. Don't ever tell me to walk away."

Fuck.

"I'm crazy, Juliette," I confess. "I've got this poison inside of me. This darkness that I don't know how to fight."

She shakes her head, tears pouring from her eyes. Seriously, between her eyes and my hand, there's blood and tears everywhere.

"Don't fight it," she whispers. "Give me your darkness. Give it to me, and I'll give mine to you. I am *never* walking away from you."

She's so fucking angry. So beautiful.

"No more secrets," she says. "I want you. All of you. Every little piece."

I walk her backwards, so her ass is resting against the wall.

"Why would you want me?" I ask her, hot water stinging my eyes. "I'm no good."

She swallows thickly, resting her hand over my heart. "Because you are good. Because you're mine. Because we belong to each other. Because I've never loved anyone the way I love you. I love you because you're *you*."

She's so angry, and I'm so fucking relieved. My beautiful girl is angry, and she's full of life again for the first time since Dornan died. And she's telling me, from the very depths of her soul, that she loves me, more than anything, even though she knows everything now.

The weighted stone that's been knotted around my heart, dragging me down every fucking day for years, breaks. I feel the weight lift, and it's terrifying. I feel like I could fly. She loves me.

And I believe her.

I push her into the wall, kissing her like I'm a dying man and she's the thing that'll save me. Because she *is* the thing that will save me. She always has been.

My beautiful, vengeful girl.

CHAPTER NINETEEN

Juliette

"We should have done this at night," Jase says, peering through the scope on the rocket launcher as he chews gum nervously.

I look through my own scope, excited and terrified of the firepower I've got in front of me. We're in four locations—Elliot in an office building that directly overlooks the side fire escape of the Gypsy Brothers clubhouse, Luis parked across the road running surveillance, Tommy crouched on the roof of a cafe behind the club, and Jase and I in a vacant second-floor apartment directly across from the main building entrance to round out the circle we've created. I love how I'm the only one who needs a partner, but Elliot's assured me it's because I'm a good aim. While Elliot,

Luis and Tommy are tasked with blowing up the building in general, Jase and I have the responsibility of wasting anyone who might seek to escape when the first round of explosive charges are fired inside the building. Each of us is wearing an earpiece and dressed in black combat wear, and I've got to say, I feel like Lara Fucking Croft right now.

Our firepower might seem like overkill, but it's for good reason—the moment the Gypsies catch sight of where they're being attacked from, they'll retaliate. And none of us are particularly keen to get shot today.

Jase is pacing nervously at the window because we're five minutes from show time. We've been here all morning, waiting for the last stragglers to arrive at the clubhouse for their weekly meeting. These motherfuckers aren't going to be chasing us anymore. We'll deal with this lot, and then we'll deal with Julian Ross and the Cartel—a slightly larger task, but we're up for it—and then we'll all finally be able to move on without fear. Without running. Without having to hide in the dark.

"Four minutes," Elliot's voice comes over the earpiece I'm wearing.

I adjust my hair. Wipe my palms on my pants. Stare outside and imagine the carnage that's about to unfold.

"Three minutes," Elliot says. Jase is sporting an identical earpiece beside me, and he steps away from his rocket launcher at the three-minute announcement, our eyes meeting.

"You look fucking beautiful right now," he says, his eyes taking in my black outfit, the long plait he put in my hair so it wouldn't get in the way, the smile I'm wearing like I'm a fucking jack-o-lantern on Halloween.

"You don't look so bad yourself," I reply, smirking as he rearranges his pants. "Don't let that thing hit the trigger by accident," I say.

He laughs, pulling me to his chest and kissing me like it's the first time he's ever laid his hands on me before. Like it's the last.

It had better fucking not be the last.

Elliot calls the last minutes out.

Two minutes.

One.

At thirty seconds, we stuff our ears full of earplugs.

At twenty seconds, I place my finger on the trigger of my rocket launcher.

Five seconds.

Four.

I take a deep breath in.

Three.

Two.

I let my breath out until there's nothing left.

One.

None. No seconds left. We all do the thing we were meant to do. We all fire in the right spots, and we don't stop unless we're reloading. We all do our job. I shoot until I lose count of how many rocket-propelled explosives I've loaded and launched. My head starts to buzz under the constant reverberation of the firing sound, the earplugs acting much like a bandaid over a bullet wound. And within five tiny, insignificant minutes, the Gypsy Brothers clubhouse has exploded in a brilliant display of orange fireballs and black smoke, and nobody is trying to run out of the exits.

We did it. We ended the Gypsy Brothers.

We're almost free.

CHAPTER TWENTY

Juliette

We're all on tenterhooks. Well, Jase and I are. I'm assuming the other three are as well, judging by the rapid breathing I can hear over the radio.

"Any movement?" I ask.

"None here," Elliot's voice crackles.

"Clear here," Tommy chimes in.

"Clear here, too," Luis says.

"We're clear in front," Jase says.

"Well, lady and gentlemen, it was a pleasure doing business," Elliot says. "We've got about two minutes to get the fuck out of here. You know what to do."

Jase rips his earpiece out and turns to me, the look on his face priceless. He looks like he's the cat that got the cream, and I must look the same, because that's how I feel.

I was wrong. Not all vengeance is hollow. I feel like, for once in so very long, I can see the light at the end of this dark tunnel.

We make quick work of breaking our weapons down—Jase has to help me with the rocket launcher, because I've forgotten already how it packs away into its bag—and then he's opening the door of the apartment, gesturing for me to wait while he checks the hallway.

I close the window we've been using to fire out of, sling my bag full of heavy artillery over my shoulder and look back to Jase. He's still framed by the open door, but he's facing away from me.

"We clear?" I whisper.

I see him press a palm to his neck as he stumbles. He looks... drunk.

"Hey!" I hiss. "Jase!"

Something doesn't feel right. Jase rounds the corner abruptly so he's in the hallway, out of my line of sight, and that's when I reach back into the bag I'm carrying to grab my gun. Weapon firmly in hand, I tentatively inch out into the hallway.

"Jase?"

He's on the ground, two feet away, knocked the fuck out. "Jase!" I say, rushing to him. Before I can get down to him, though, something presses over my face. A hand. A hand wrapped in a leather glove. A second hand grabs my wrist - the one attached to my gun-holding hand—and bends it back until I lose my grip on the butt of the gun. It falls to the ground and the mystery attacker's foot kicks it away, sending it in the opposite direction of an unconscious Jase. Fuck!

A strong arm wraps around my waist and yanks me backward. The leather-covered hand presses tightly against my nose and mouth, cutting off every bit of air. I freeze for a split second, like a deer in headlights, and then I go wild. The hallway is narrow, allowing me to kick my legs up and brace my heels on the wall for a moment before I push back with every ounce of strength I possess. Whoever has hold of me is at least a head taller than me, so I push back and up, smashing the back of my head against the nose of my captor with a satisfying crunch. I groan, seeing stars as the arms around me loosen enough for me to slide down and out of their crushing grip.

I stay low, crawling on my hands and knees until I'm clear, and then I get to my feet, turning to see my attacker. He's white. Mid-forties. Wearing a suit and tie that look like they've seen better days. And he's got a strange-looking gun slung over his shoulder. It's long and skinny and has animal stickers plastered all up the barrel.

"Who the fuck are you?" I ask.

Behind him, another figure steps out of the apartment next to the one we were just in. *Oh, shit.*

"It doesn't matter who he is," Julian Ross says, smiling wide as he steps over Jase like he's not even there. "What matters is who I am. You remember me, Juliette?"

I take him in as I assess the situation: we're fucked. Unless I can take on both of these guys, we are royally fucked. Julian Ross looks as sharp as ever, a younger version of his dead brother Emilio. He's got the same dark eyes and Italian features the males of this family share, but his face is more craggy and lined with a difficult life, his nose larger and crooked, his hair fairer and his fingers adorned with gold rings. He looks like your typical Mafioso, dripping in gold and Armani.

I open my mouth to answer him, but no words come out. Because there's something stinging my neck, like a wasp driving its tail into my flesh.

I put my hand to my neck, feeling something thin and hard. Trying not to gag, I pull at the plastic until it comes away in my hand.

A tranquilizer dart. Now I get why the guy's gun looks weird. It's a tranquilizer gun, designed for taking down a dog or a small bear.

"You feeling okay, Miss Portland?" Julian asks, coming closer. Coming for me. My vision starts to blur as I look between the dart in my hand and the man rapidly closing in on me.

I open my mouth. I close my mouth. I crumple like an accordion, falling flat on my back. My legs are useless, my arms tingling, my universe spinning.

Julian peers over me. "Have a nice little sleep, won't you? We're about to take a little trip, you and me."

Fffffffuuuuuuck!

Darkness.

I gasp.

I was asleep, like completely unconscious, and now something cold and wet is being poured over my head, running into my eyes and dribbling between my breasts.

I come to painfully, blinking to get the water out of my eyes. At least I hope it's water and not gasoline or something. I bring my hands up to wipe my eyes and find them bound together with a zip-tie that's cutting into my skin. Great.

I shake water droplets from my face and look around, taking in my surroundings. I'm in the back of a limousine, sitting upright in a plush leather seat. Jase is to my left, trying to wipe the water from his own eyes. His hands are bound in his lap as well, and we've both been relieved of our weapons by the looks of things.

"You're so cute when you sleep," Julian Ross says to me, his brown eyes flat and reptilian-looking. He looks like one of those gators from fucking Miami, roaming the canals in search of fresh meat. He's sitting across from me, his sidekick in the bad suit next to him.

Jase goes to launch himself at Julian, but Julian holds his finger up in warning, a gun materializing in his other hand. It's pointed at me.

"Uh-uh," he cautions. Jase sits back in his seat, breathing heavily. I glance at him, seeing a man who's about to lose his fucking shit and rip Julian apart with his bound hands and bare teeth, even if it earns him a bullet.

"What do you want?" I ask Julian. "If you want to shoot us, hurry up and shoot us. I'm not in the mood for bullshit small talk."

Wow. I can't believe that just came out of my mouth. And yet, it did. I'm afraid, but more than that, I'm fucking furious.

Julian laughs. "So much anger for somebody so small," he says. "Somebody so helpless."

"What.Do.You.Want?" I repeat.

He runs his tongue along his teeth. "You know what I want. I want what your daddy took. I want my money."

"Your money?" I repeat dully. "We just wiped out your entire biker club. Your means to move your drugs, and your weapons, and your cash. But you don't want to make us pay, or punish us, or anything else like that—you just want your money?"

I sigh. "I've got to say, I'm a little underwhelmed."

I'm stalling. I don't have a clear plan here, so I'm stalling, hoping someone will spring us, hoping for a fucking miracle. Stalling so he doesn't shoot us both right now.

"Ah, but you did me a favor," Julian replies, grinning. "I'm a different operator than my brother was. I don't like sharing. And I don't like dirty bikers getting in my business. So thank you. You just saved me a real headache."

"You're so welcome," I say sarcastically. "Maybe you could let us go as a gesture of your gratitude."

Julian's eyes narrow. "And maybe you could get your scheming little ass out of this car and take a little walk into the bank with me."

I glance out of my window to see a large building in front of us. Of course. We're in downtown Los Angeles, in the banking district.

"A little bird tells me you've got a safety deposit box here, Miss Portland."

"Let him go," I lift my chin towards Jase, "and I'll get you whatever you want from that bank."

Julian shifts forward, placing the barrel of his gun against Jase's left thigh.

"This is not a negotiation," he breathes. "I'm going to free your hands, both of you. You're going to get out of this car with me, and you're going to walk into that bank, and get me that fucking safety deposit box. We're going to open it, and you're not going to make a scene. Because if you do, I start killing my nephew's traitorous fucking son here that you seem to be so fond of."

"You're going to kill us anyway," Jase says. "Why would we help you first?"

Julian cocks the hammer of his gun and digs it harder into Jase's thigh.

"You remember the little video of your girlfriend? The snufftastic gang bang of Juliette Portland? You remember that, don't you, Jason?"

Jase's nostrils flare as he breathes heavily, his eyes bugging out as he watches the gun in his leg.

"You make this difficult for me, and I'll make volume two. Juliette goes to pound town. Juliette gets fucked by every member of my Cartel. Juliette's asshole goes for a ride to Mexico. Are you picking up what I'm putting down, boy?"

Jase looks like he's about to burst a blood vessel. Julian sits back and smiles, the guy beside him producing a small box-cutter. "Hands," Julian orders, and Jase and I reluctantly stick our bound hands out. The guy who tranquilized us cuts through our bindings.

"Play nice, you two," Julian warns as he knocks on his window and the door opens. He steps out, draping his jacket over his arm to conceal his gun.

I look at Jase. He looks back at me, regret written all over his face.

I want to tell him not to worry. That we'll find a way out.

But I don't.

Because I don't know how we're going to get out of *this.*

CHAPTER TWENTY-ONE

Juliette

Ten minutes later, we're inside the vault that houses every safety deposit box in this bank. A security guard stands just outside the door.

Julian stands beside me, pressing a key into my outstretched palm. Jase is on the other side of the room with tranquillizer dude, who didn't manage to smuggle his large dart gun into the bank. The only weapon in the room is Julian's gun, and I know Jase is thinking exactly the same thing as me: How the fuck to get it away from him.

I take a deep breath. Number three-fifty-three. I locate the box, about waist height and off to my right, and I slide the key in, turning it with a trepidatious breath.

It clicks and the long metal box releases, allowing me to pull it out of its spot. I slide it out, turning to place it on the square table that takes up the center of the room.

"Open it," Julian says, his gun pointed at me. How he got it this far into the bank undetected is beyond me. He must have paid the guard off or something.

I open it, marveling at how razor-sharp the long lid of the box edge is as my life flashes before my eyes. Everything is just as I left it the morning before I went back to find Dornan and begin my wreck and ruin of his universe. There's my passport, some photographs, and a small stack of hundred dollar bills.

Emphasis on small. Julian peers over, doing a double take when he sees how little money is in front of him.

"Is this some kind of fucking joke?" he asks, snatching the stack of hundreds up and flipping through it. "There's maybe four hundred grand in here. Where's the rest of it?!"

I shrug petulantly. "How the fuck should I know? This is all I've ever seen."

He throws the stack down on the table in front of me and makes a growling noise in the back of his throat. He grabs the back of my head and slams my face into the table. *Jesus!*

My ears ring and I taste blood on my tongue. I hope he hasn't knocked any of my teeth loose. My mouth bears the brunt of the impact, sparing my ten thousand dollar nose job.

"Hey!" Jase yells from across the table. Julian points his gun at him in warning. "I wouldn't if I were you. I will shoot you dead and piss on your dead body, you fucking traitor."

Julian fists his hand in my hair and pulls me back to my feet.

"Where's my money," he hisses. "There should be ten times that amount there!"

I raise my eyebrows. "How the hell should I know? I didn't take it."

He takes a deep breath and licks his lips, studying my face.

"Five million dollars," he says, trailing a finger over my shoulder. "I wonder how many snuff movies I'd have to make of you to make *five million dollars*."

"Get your fucking hands off her, old man," Jase snaps.

Julian looks over at Jase like he's a dead cockroach stuck to his expensive Italian loafer, reaching over and pinching my nipple at the same time.

"Ah!" I cry, stepping backwards. *What am I going to do?* I refuse to let this fucker kill me after everything we've been through.

Julian looks back to me. "You step back again and I'll shoot you in your pretty fucking face," he says.

"Won't get your five million then, will you old man."

He breathes angrily. "Fine. You step back again and I'll shoot your boy in *his* pretty fucking face. And then you'll be my new baby porn star. And I'll make sure you die a slow, painful death after you've earned out the cash your daddy stole from us."

"What are you going to make me do?" I ask. Stalling, always stalling. Where's my fucking back-up crew? Where's my fucking miracle?

Julian smiles. "Lots of things."

"Tell me," I say defiantly. "I want to know what you've got planned for me."

He narrows his eyes at me, suspicion written all over his face. "Why?"

I shrug. "Because maybe I like doing dirty things. Maybe you won't have to kill me. *Maybe* you'll decide you like me enough to keep me. Dornan was never going to kill me. He was going to keep me because I'm *that* good."

Julian's eyebrows rise. "Can you believe this bitch?" He asks the other dude, who looks about as interested as I feel. He whips his gaze back to me. "What makes you think you're so good?"

"You've seen the video, surely," I reply. "There's plenty more where that came from."

"You're a fucking liar."

"No, I'm not," I reply. "Get your camera phone out, old man, and I'll get on my knees and suck your cock right now. We can be making money on porntube tonight."

"Juliette!" Jase says.

"Fuck you, Jase. I saw you screwing that girl last night at the club while you thought I wasn't watching." I stare at him, widening my eyes. *Go along with me, Jase. For God's sake, go along with me.*

"Don't fucking touch her, Julian," Jase warns.

But Julian looks excited. A pretty young girl is offering to suck his cock and let him record it. In a bank vault. At one o clock in the afternoon.

I glance at the empty safety-deposit box on the table. My hands are itching to grab it. It's so sharp! Maybe that's my miracle, after all.

"How do I know you're not going to bite me?" Julian asks.

I shrug. "Well, you've got a gun, big shot. I'm not about to bite you and get a bullet in my brain."

He's hesitant.

"Come on, old man. Get your phone out and start taping."

"Juliette!" Jase yells.

I don't respond. I'm balanced on the balls of my feet, ready to move at a second's notice. I put one hand on the table beside me, almost a casual move, as Julian reaches into his pocket to pull out his phone.

He lowers his aim for one fucking second. And I take my chance.

Picking up the metal safety-deposit box, I smash it into Julian's gun. He grunts and his fingers lose grip, the gun skidding across the floor.

"You cunt!" he yells, going to tackle me. I don't let him get that far, though. I swipe the sharp edge of the safety-deposit box lid across his throat as hard as I can, a bright slash of blood appearing at his neck.

Julian's hands go to his throat immediately as arterial blood sprays me in the face. "Ugh," I moan, spitting the taste of his blood out of my mouth. I look to my left to see Jase and the guard struggling over the gun.

Oh, fuck. They've both got a grip on it. As I'm watching them, Julian makes another clumsy grab for me. I raise the box again, smashing it into his face so he drops to his knees. He's bleeding everywhere, spraying the wall of safety deposit boxes with lashings of blood as his heart tries to pump in vain.

"Should have let us walk away, old man," I say, lifting the edge of the box lid above my head and driving it into the fleshy part of his neck. It finds purchase, stopping when it hits bone, and Julian Ross is dead, his mouth and eyes frozen open.

I turn my attention to Jase and the guy rolling around on the floor just as Jase gets the upper hand, pinning the guy beneath him and smashing the butt of the gun into his face until he passes out. Jase holds the guy's nose and covers his mouth for almost a full minute until he lifts off the floor ever so slightly and then goes limp. I don't interrupt. It's stressful enough killing someone without trying to have conversation at the same time. Then, as Jase is standing up and I'm anxiously looking around for any cameras that might be in this room, the door bursts open. The security guard who was flanking the door to the vault rushes in, his own weapon drawn and pointed at Jase. I don't even give him a chance to see me. I fly at him from the side, knocking the gun from his hand. It skids underneath the table, out of immediate reach. I kick the door shut with my foot and lean against it, catching my breath.

The security guard's eyes go wide and I give him a warning look when he looks like he's going to yell for help.

"Wouldn't do that," I say, glancing at his name tag. "Herb

Trasker. Are there cameras in this room, Herb?"

He gulps nervously, shaking his head. Herb is sweating profusely. He's about a hundred pounds overweight, and I'm afraid he's going to die of a heart attack if we don't reel this in quickly.

"You like money, Herb?" I ask, looking at Jase to see he's still got Julian's gun trained on the guard.

Herb doesn't answer. I motion to the stack of bills on the table. "A hundred grand, Herb, if you let us walk. What do you say? We're not bank robbers. We're not bad people. We're just trying to get through the day."

Herb looks at the money anxiously, licking his lips.

"You got a family, herb?" Jason cuts in. "Get his wallet."

Herb's face falls at the mention of family. "Please," he says. "I've got a newborn baby girl. A wife. Please don't bring my family into this. I'm just trying to get through the day, too."

I nod. "You got your car keys on you, Herb?"

He nods. "Do you need a getaway car?"

I smile. "That we do, Herb. A getaway car and your jacket to clean this blood off my face. No silly moves or my partner here will shoot you. He *really* wants to shoot somebody today."

Jase smiles congenially at poor Herb.

Herb shrugs out of his jacket reluctantly and hands it to me. I wipe my face as best I can, hoping there's nothing too obvious. We just need to get across the parking lot and we'll be set.

Herb reluctantly hands over his keys, cell phone and wallet. I smile, thanking him as I hand back his blood-smeared jacket.

"It was nice meeting you, Herb."

He opens his mouth to say something, but he doesn't get the chance. Jase hits him over the head with the butt of Julian's gun, and he goes down hard. I scoop up the money and the photographs and stuff them in Jase's pockets.

"Blood check?" I ask Jase, turning my head so he can see both sides of my face. He grimaces. "Yeah. On your teeth. Just don't open your mouth. And definitely don't kiss me."

I laugh.

We don't have any trouble exiting the bank, much to my surprise. After clicking the remote on Herb's keychain a few times, Jase points. "The Civic. Over there."

We take Herb's car, after we kill the limo driver with a single shot to the head and collect our rocket launchers. For a major financial district, nobody seems to have noticed the triple homicide that's just taken place. I guess we just don't look that threatening.

While Jase takes the wheel, I call Elliot and let him know where to meet us. They've been searching for us since they realized we were MIA, and Elliot sounds like he's almost crying when we end the call.

When we get to our destination, Jase parks the car and we get out, taking our things with us. Two rocket launchers, broken down and stowed in long canvas bags. A couple handguns that we hide with the rocket launchers. My passport. And a stack of photos that I've been waiting to go back to for months.

I knock on the door and wait. A few moments later, a woman answers the door. She's holding a baby in her arms, a chubby little thing that looks just like Herb, only a lot cuter. I smile at the woman broadly, sticking my hand out.

"Mrs. Trasker?" I ask. She takes my hand slowly, looking puzzled.

"Can I help you?" she asks.

"We're friends of Herb's," Jase says, flashing her a dazzling smile as he hands her Herb's car keys. "We're here to drop his car off. Please tell him we left his work files in the backseat for him.

She looks from me to Jase, confusion all over her face. "Do you work at the bank?" she asks.

"We're consultants," Jase says. "Please tell him about the work files in the backseat. They're very important. Very time-sensitive."

I wonder how Herb's going to react when he sees that we kept our promise—that he's got a stash of cash in his car that will set him up for life.

Five minutes later, the three musketeers—Luis, Elliot and Tommy—pull up in the Hummer Elliot rented. Lucky we have fake credit cards, because otherwise Avis is going to stop letting us rent cars. Because we never seem to manage to take them back. They keep getting left in airfields or apartment parking lots.

We get into the backset with Luis. Elliot's driving, and Tommy's shotgun. As soon as we're safely shut into the car, Elliot speeds away up the street. We don't need Mrs. Trasker getting our plate number.

"How about a high fucking five!" Tommy yells, twisting in his seat and holding out his palm to us. I laugh, high-fiving him. Jase shakes his head in embarrassment, but doesn't leave Tommy hanging.

Elliot turns around and flashes me a smug grin, before looking back to the road. Luis is pouring a shot of tequila down his throat, before offering me the bottle. I take a swig, figuring it'll disinfect my mouth of Julian's blood, if nothing else. Jase reaches out and grabs my hand, squeezing it tightly. Impulsively, I turn and kiss him full on the mouth, and he kisses me back, almost devouring me.

"Oh, get a fucking room, you two," Elliot says, but when I meet his eyes in the rearview mirror, he's practically beaming. He's happy.

We're all happy.

We're *free*.

CHAPTER TWENTY-TWO

Juliette

One week later

"Jesus," Tommy groans. "This thing weighs a fucking ton."

He's struggling to carry the large framed painting I asked him to grab from Dornan's office—my fathers old office—in Va Va Voom. I couldn't bear to go back, after every thing that happened there. It was where they attacked me. And, six years later, it was the place where I went back to find my revenge.

"It's just canvas and wood," I say, coming over to inspect it. I smile, pressing my palm against the thin layer of glass that protects the painting inside. It's something my father brought home when I was a little girl. A painting of a beach in Maui that he used to talk about all the time.

It was the place he was going to take me, and Jase, and Mariana.

I try to lift the painting, and Tommy's right—it's much heavier than it should be. I turn it over, puzzled, running my fingers along the thick brown paper that covers the back of it. There's a small tear in the back, about the size of a five-cent piece, and I peer inside.

"Oh yeah, sorry," Tommy says. "I dropped it on the desk. Can we tape it up or something?"

I tilt my head, a strange feeling washing over me as I realize what I'm seeing through that tiny tear in the paper.

"We could tape it up," I reply, ripping the paper to expose what's stacked underneath. "Don't think we should, though."

Elliot, who's rocking on a dining chair and eating an apple, stops mid-chew and stands up so fast, his chair crashes to the floor. "What the—" he says around his mouth full of fruit.

Jase and Luis look over from the heated game they're fighting over on the PlayStation. "What is it?" Jase says.

I rip the rest of the paper off and grab the first stack of bills, holding it up.

"Cash money."

Jase and Luis drop their game controllers and come over, one on each side of me as we stare down at the obscene amount of cash.

"This is what they were looking for," Jase says. "What they were all looking for, this whole time."

"Christ, how much is here?" Tommy asks. Elliot picks up a stack and thumbs through it. "A hundred grand in each bundle," he says.

I try to count all of the stacks of bills and I get to twenty before I lose track and have to start again.

"Fifty-three," Jase says.

"Five hundred thousand?" Tommy asks.

Jase looks at him like he's an idiot. "No," he says slowly, "Five *million* dollars."

Five million dollars. Dornan and his family looked for this money for years, and all along it was right in front of them. Dornan looked this money every single day, and he didn't even know.

I laugh. I pick up handfuls of the money and I laugh and laugh and laugh.

CHAPTER TWENTY-THREE

Juliette

One month later

I woke because I could hear thunder off the coast, and I wanted to see if there was lightning. Jase and I fell asleep early, and now I'm wide awake. I guess my body is accustomed to having scarce sleep, and it keeps waking me up at weird hours. Or maybe it's because we're in a different time zone again. Its three a.m. here in Montauk, a small coastal town a couple hours drive from New York City. We've been here for a few weeks now, in Elliot's old beach shack, which sits directly on the water. It's so different to the beaches in Los Angeles, but it still feels familiar. Safe. I feel safe here.

I have gained five pounds, and I already look healthier.

I am eating. I am sleeping. I am smiling.

I am in love.

I stare out of the window at the ocean, shivering. I'm barefoot, wearing a white sleeveless dress that falls to my ankles and makes my red hair look like blood against the crisp fabric. Since we've been here, I've bought myself a whole new wardrobe online and had it shipped here. It's not that I don't want to go outside, but Jase and I have been busy getting to know each other again. We've spent a lot of time on the beach, and the rest of it in bed. We've learned quickly to be quiet, because we're staying with Elliot and his little family, and the last thing I need is Elliot's three year old to ask me why I was screaming during the night.

I hear movement behind me and turn to see Jase is awake, leaning on one elbow as he watches me from our bed.

"Did I wake you?" I whisper.

He shakes his head. "I was just thinking."

I smile, crawling back into bed beside him. "About what?"

"About you," he says, grabbing my hips and pulling me on top of him.

"That's what you always say," I reply, shifting as he pulls my panties to the side and presses two fingers inside me.

I tip my head back, moaning softly as he adds a third finger.

"You're so tight," he says, sliding his fingers in and out of my wet heat. I can feel his erection growing underneath me, and I reach down to pull his boxers down and grab his thick shaft.

"Jesus," he says, as I start to stroke him. "I think you've already taken everything. My balls are empty."

I raise my eyebrows. "I highly doubt that." A few more stokes and a bead of premium appears on the tip, glistening and ready. "See?" I smirk. I push his hand away from my pussy, immediately feeling the empty space his fingers left, throbbing with need. I smile as I wrap my hand around his hard length and guide him to my entrance.

"I don't want to hurt you," Jase says, his eyes glazed.

"Yes you do," I murmur as I sink down on top of him, so I'm filled with him. Flames of desire lick across my belly, reaching all the way down to my clit, where I've got one finger, circling myself as I stay still on Jase.

"You want to hurt me, and I want you to hurt me. And that's okay."

His fingers dig into my arms. He still struggles at the start. He doesn't know how to let go very easily.

"I want to fuck you so hard," he says, his fingers bruising me. "I want to tie you to the bedhead and fuck you until you scream."

I smile wickedly. Just the thought of him doing that—tying me up so I'm completely at his mercy—it's got me wetter than I've ever been. I feel like I could come without moving, just sitting here, impaled on his thick shaft as he promises me all the darkness in his soul.

"What else," I murmur, as I start to move my hips ever-so-slightly, creating the most delicious heat between us. The most unbearable anticipation of what he might do to me.

He leans over and pulls my dress down so my breasts pop out, my nipples already hard in the cool night air.

"I'll have to gag you," he says, tracing a line down my chin. "We can't wake the others."

I smile wider, biting my lip. This is hot. It's so fucking hot.

"What else?" I press.

He takes one nipple into his mouth and bites down on it, making me shudder. It hurts, but it's a good hurt.

"I want to tie your hands behind your back and fuck your mouth until you choke on me," he says.

I imagine being on my knees, my throat full of him, wanting to rub my clit while I suck his cock, the thrill of not having my hands to touch myself. The powerlessness. I can't wait. For all of it, I can't wait. I'm so wet, I can feel my pussy leaking over his cock.

"Anything else?"

He pulls away from my tits and grips the back of my neck with one hand. Clutches the front with the other.

"I want to choke you until you come," he says, sounding unsure this time, his expression anguished.

"Good," I say. "Let's start with that. Because I'm about to come, and then I'm going to suck your cock until you come in my mouth."

"Fuck," he groans, jutting his hips up to create friction between us. "Do you have any idea how fucking hot you sound right now?"

And then doubt crosses his face and he stops, his hand at the front of my neck loosening.

"I don't want to hurt you," he says, his voice full of doubt and lust.

"I trust you," I whisper. "I love you. *Do it*."

And that's all it takes to break his doubt. Love, trust, and the knowledge that I want this.

His hand tightens around my neck, and that's all it takes. His thumbs pressing into the base of my throat, his thrusts harder and faster, and I break, tightening around his cock as I orgasm. As I see nothing but his dark eyes and a burst of white stars.

As he takes my breath away.

As I let him.

I don't have time to catch my breath before Jase has me on my knees, my dress torn off and hands tied behind my back with a pair of panties. I'm still seeing white, still cresting down the aftermath of the orgasm he just ripped from me, when I feel the fat tip of his cock press against my lips. I open my mouth; greedy to taste the bead of pre-cum I can see glistening on the tip. It's salty, making my mouth come alive, saliva rushing in to lubricate my tongue. My pussy clenches when he fists my hair and pushes himself against the back of my throat, making me gag.

He doesn't stop fucking my mouth. He knows I'll bite down ever-so-gently if I need him to stop. And right now, I do not want him to stop. I'm so turned on by the way he's thrusting over my tongue, I can hardly bear it.

"Jesus," Jase says. "Your mouth is so good. So good. I want to wrap your dress around your neck while I come in your mouth."

I blink once for yes, and the dress materializes in his hand. He stops moving for a moment, letting me catch my breath. I take several deep breaths, my pussy vibrating with desire, my clit screaming for some kind of attention.

The dress goes around my throat.

He starts moving again, hitting the back of my throat and pulling the material around my neck tight at the same time. I can only get tiny sips of air, and only when he pulls back, and only for a moment before his cock slides into my mouth again.

Just when I think he's going to come, he pulls out of my mouth abruptly and yanks on the dress, forcing me to my feet. He drags me to the bed, throwing me down on my back and forcing my knees apart so wide, my hips scream in protest. He slams into me so hard I scream. A silent scream, because his tongue is already in my mouth, kissing me greedily.

He's fucking me so hard I'm moving up the bed with each stroke. I'll be hurting tomorrow, but I don't care. All I care about is this moment, this very second, with the boy I love.

We lost each other once.

We almost lost each other twice.

We'll never lose each other again.

Afterwards, I shower and put pajamas on. It gets cold here at night, so I've got long pants and a tank top to sleep in. They might survive the night if Jase doesn't rip them off. Depends how tired he is.

I don't care. We've got plenty of money to buy new pajamas, and nowhere to be in the morning.

Tears fill my eyes as I watch Mother Nature's light show from the deck. I'm not scared. I'm just… happy.

Jase sees my glassy eyes. "What's wrong?" he asks, squeezing my hand.

I shake my head. "Nothing," I say, almost in wonderment. "Not one thing."

A smile lights up his face, going all the way to his dark eyes. *There he is.* The boy I love. He was always there, underneath the shame and the weight of his own past, but now he's here, with me, and finally, we don't have to run anymore.

"Can you believe we made it?" I ask, a tear dripping onto my cheek. "Can you believe we made it out of there alive?"

Jase pulls me towards him, kissing me, and behind us the sky lights up the darkness.

CHAPTER TWENTY-FOUR

Elliot

There's an old fishing shack in the Hamptons that my parents used to take me to before they died. It's one of those bare bones places; raw timber walls, four tin plates, a cupboard full of old newspapers to light up and kindle the open fire.

You can see the beach from every room in the house, which means the bare bunk beds don't feel quite so hard; the old Adirondack chairs don't feel so splintered.

My mother would pack our old Mustang with cold-cut sandwiches and Cokes and cushions. That's all she took. We'd each live in our bathing suits, me and my sister and our parents.

Then they died, and we got the shack in their will, but I've never been back since.

I didn't want to come back. Didn't want to see the goddamn place. Because it was so innocent, and so good, and I was afraid that if I came back it'd be less than perfect.

It was Ames who urged me to come back. To bring Kayla and make some memories of our own. So I did. And she was right. It's perfect for us.

It's perfect, but it's time for us to move on, for now at least. The Gypsy Brothers are gone, the Cartel is in ruins and our DEA contact has mysteriously vanished without a trace. When Luis told me he'd handled Fitz, I didn't quite know how, but I didn't think I should ask.

I imagine he's taking a nice, long swim in the Atlantic somewhere.

Tommy's back in San Francisco, and that's where we're headed, too. Amy has family there, a new job opportunity with the SFPD, and it's my turn to follow her somewhere and help her out with Kayla while she does something for her career. I mean, she's spent long enough following me around the country while a bloodthirsty drug cartel tried to kill us all, so I figure I owe her that much. Amy and I, we're not together—but we're a family, and we still get along, and we're sticking tight while Kayla's young and she needs two parents.

Plus, I'll admit—I don't want to let either of them out of my sight for the rest of my life.

The car is packed. Amy has already carried a sleeping Kayla into the garage and settled her in her car seat. Now, it's time to lock the door, start the car, and begin our road trip. For once, we're not running. It's our choice to move to San Francisco, and something about it feels so exciting, so different, that I'm wide awake and chipper at the ass-crack of dawn.

I walk past Jase and Juliette's room, noticing the door's slightly ajar. I wonder if we've woken them with our noise. But when I poke my head into the room, the moonlight slicing through the curtains shows me two bodies curled tightly together under the duvet, fast asleep.

I watch for a moment, the steady rise and fall of their chests, the way her arm is thrown over his, and I smile.

They're sleeping. Actually sleeping. Both of them.

I grin, shaking my head in wonder as I close and lock the front. In the garage, Amy is waiting for me, holding out a thermos of coffee. She's the only one who's ever been able to make it just the way I like. Fuck, if it weren't for the fact that we start fighting whenever we start screwing each other, I'd say I should marry this girl. For now, I'll take having her as my best friend and the mother of my daughter.

"Thanks," I say, taking the coffee and tipping it down my throat. It's boiling hot and I'm freezing cold, so it works extremely well to warm me up.

"You excited?" Amy asks, glancing back at Kayla before settling her attention on me. I smile, setting the thermos in the cup holder that sits in between us.

"To move to Vegas and gamble every day? Hell yeah." I gun the engine and press the button on the garage remote, waiting as the door lifts up.

"You wish, buddy," Amy says, hitting me playfully.

"Ow!" I say, pushing her hand away. "Stop trying to touch my junk."

"You wish I would touch your junk," she replies. I laugh as I back out of the garage and onto the road.

"The important thing is that the invitation is always open, Ames," I say, putting the car into gear and driving away.

"Are we going to talk about your junk for the entire trip?" Amy asks, sipping her coffee.

"That depends," I reply. "You want to play I spy?"

Amy rolls her eyes, but she's smiling. "Is it something beginning with D?"

I feign surprise. "How'd you guess?"

She just snort-laughs, shaking her head at me. I smile, glancing at our beautiful daughter in the rearview mirror.

It is so fucking good to be driving somewhere when you're not being chased.

As I'm getting onto the expressway, I think about Juliette. I think about the girl who almost died in front of me all those years ago, and the girl I just saw sleeping in my family's beach shack ten minutes ago, and my chest floods with pride. All those years I tried to make her better, and she's finally, finally okay.

Better than okay. She's… shining. Yeah. She's the girl I saw glimpses of underneath all the hurt and the fear and the bullshit. I knew she'd be like that. Funny. Beautiful. Smart. She's finally found herself after all these years.

She's finally found her peace.

And, in some strange way, she's helped me find mine.

EPILOGUE

Eight years ago

The girl was afraid at first, but her curiosity won out over her fear. She'd seen her uncle drag the boy in, unconscious and covered in blood, and she'd listened from the next room as they held him down and tattooed something across his back.

She crept into the room he'd been thrown into, seeing his back first. He was sitting on the edge of the bed, facing away from the door with his head in his hands. His back was covered in blood and black ink, swollen and red from where they'd just dragged needles through his flesh. And he was crying.

He must have seen her out of the corner of his eye, jumping suddenly and turning on her. He looked angry. Enraged. Terrified.

She didn't move. She'd never met him before, but she knew who he was as soon as she saw his dark, anguished eyes. He had to be Dornan's son. He looked a couple years older than her, and he was completely and utterly broken.

"Are you okay?" she'd whispered, edging closer. His expression was wild. He couldn't talk. He couldn't form words. Her heart hurt as she watched him try.

She sat on the narrow bed beside him and reached out a hand.

"I promise not to hurt you," she said, leaving her hand there on the bed between them, an invitation for if and when he was ready.

He shied away. He looked like he might try and run.

But he surprised her. He took her hand.

She smiled, squeezing ever-so-gently.

"It's going to be okay," she whispered.

She loved him, even then. Her beautiful broken boy.

He didn't smile. He didn't blink.

But he squeezed her hand back.

And she knew, somehow, that they belonged to each other.

GYPSY BROTHERS

ALTERNATE

A word from the author:

I wrote ALTERNATE as a chance for my readers to take a glimpse into the psyche and inner workings of my main male characters: After mourning the end of the Gypsy Brothers series (or, what I thought was the end), I'm THRILLED to be able to dip back into the minds of these dark and delicious men. From the brutality of Dornan Ross, to the tenacity and love of Elliot McRae, and the shattering secrets that Jason Ross harbours deep inside his soul, these stories flew from my fingertips faster than I could type.

If you're easily offended (who the fuck am I kidding? You just finished the GYPSY BROTHERS series), I wouldn't read this. Because if you think you know these men, especially Jase?

You have no idea.

Love,
Lili

ALTERNATE

Dornan

The moment Samantha Peyton walks into my office, I want to fuck her. More than that, I want to wrap my fingers around her throat and fuck her until she passes out on my desk. I see the resemblance and my chest constricts like I'm having a heart attack. *Goddamn*. She looks like a dead woman—a dead woman who ripped my fuckin' heart out.

Mariana.

As soon as I notice the resemblance, it's gone; like a flicker of a memory I've tried to drown in blood and whores for far too long.

She's a pretty girl; young, and probably stupid like the rest of them. Before she even opens her mouth, I see a hunger in her bright blue eyes—so vivid, they almost look fake—but more than that, she looks familiar, and she feels fuckin' dangerous.

Now that can't be right … or can it? I'm the danger around here, because I *own* this town, just like I'll own this little bitch faster than she can open her mouth to say please. Before she turns around to let me fuck her in her tight, round ass, I've already decided I'm going to keep her. I'm going to use her until I can snuff out that light in her eyes and replace it with the kind of despair that will make me come like a fucking freight train when I press her face into my desk and make her beg me to stop.

The first time I fuck her? It's brutal. It's the same with every woman I get my dick wet with. I don't hurt them as a side effect. I fuck them to hurt them, and if they bleed, it's even better. Blood and pain and fucking are so inexplicably linked for me, that I'll take a woman to the brink of death just to make myself feel alive for that split-second of release. So I rear back and slam my cock into this little bitch's ass, again and again, not caring if anyone hears the sound our skin makes when it slaps together or the stunned little gasps coming from her mouth as she tries to hide how much I'm hurting her. Her pain is my pleasure.

When I finally reach breaking point and come inside her, I slam her head against my desk one last time, to daze her, to hurt her, but most of all to show her who's in fucking charge here. She might have walked in off the street thinking she was the one in control, but now that I've marked her, she's mine.

As she's leaving, I realize she's the first girl I've properly fucked in this office—John's old stomping grounds. Normally I save that shit for the Gypsy Brothers clubhouse, where as President, I've got the pick of every whore I've allowed into my inner sanctum. Whores that aren't allowed to just walk in off the street and lean their elbows on my desk as they present their pert little asses to me. Whores aren't allowed to say no, because if they do, it only makes me more determined to take what's mine. Because this whole fuckin' town is mine.

If I'd known she was here to overthrow me when she first arrived, to pick off my sons one by one until they were all dead, I would have pressed the bitch down on my desk and shoved a Glock in her mouth instead of my dick in her ass. I would have shot a bullet into her pretty face and left her face down in a dumpster. At least, that's what I think I'd do.

Hindsight is a motherfucker, ain't it? When you're dying, when your whole life flashes before your eyes, you start to wonder where you could have stopped things from going so monumentally wrong. There was a night, six years ago, when I could have stopped things.

But since that didn't happen, there was another moment. When she opened her mouth and told me her fake name—Samantha Peyton—I'd looked at her fake ID and thought, *no fucking way*. If I'd been smarter, if I'd figured out it was John's fucking kid standing in front of me, then yeah, sure. Maybe I would have killed her. Most likely.

Now? In hindsight? I would have handed the bitch my gun, pointed it at my head and told her to go to town. I mean, that's where we ended up anyway, right? Each fighting to destroy the other. I hated her. I loathed her, but I couldn't forget the little girl I'd taken home from the hospital and treated like my own. I couldn't shake the knowledge that gnawed at me deep down where it was murky and rancid.

When something seems too good to be true, it probably is. My father taught me that..

I should have listened to him.

I should be fuckin' dead right now. A lesser man would be, but there's a very clear reason I'm still alive. I feel the sorrow coursing through my veins, the undeniable fucking rage that threatens to splinter me apart, piece by torturous piece. The same way those dirty homemade bombs ripped two of my sons apart and killed them, landing two more of them in the hospital. I should be there, with them, watching over them like a good father would.

I've never claimed to be a good father, but I am a ferocious one. I always said to Celia that the day Chad came into the world was the day the beast inside me was awakened and cranked to fucking eleven. I would kill for my boys—I would die for my boys.

My boys started dying though, and I didn't have anyone to kill. I was too fucking stupid to realize their murderer was right beside me—right underneath me—as I pounded into her mercilessly, her blood spilling on my sheets as I drove my desperate grief and anger inside her.

I had no idea she was the one.

But as of an hour ago, I found out that the little harlot in my bed I called Sammi, and John's dead daughter, Juliette, are the same fucking person.

I'm more than slightly fucking embarrassed that she's been right under my nose for months … mortified, actually. Shame makes me vengeful. It's a dirty emotion. I don't want it inside me, clamouring up my black soul, making me feel like a royal fuck up, but I did. I can only blame myself. I was mesmerized by golden ass and magical pussy.

I didn't even run a proper background check on Samantha fucking Peyton.

Samantha Peyton is actually dead, turns out. She's buried in a family plot somewhere in the middle of fucking nowhere. She died in a car accident years ago and my dear little Juliette stole her identity when she decided to come back to L.A. and fuck me, good and proper.

I killed her six years ago. That night I took the girl I'd considered a daughter and turned her into my victim. I haven't had a night of solid sleep since. She died because of me.

Only she didn't fucking die.

"Sammi," I say.

She's standing in front of me now, pretty little cockroach in a tight t-shirt that shows her tits and jeans that hug her ass, and *she doesn't know I know*. For the first time in a very long time, I have the upper hand. How ironic is it that I thought I had it all along, but that's my fault for letting my dick rule my mind. The uneasiness that spread through my gut the first time I saw her pretty blue eyes should have been the tip-off, but my cock's a powerful thing. Wouldn't be the first time it led me astray. I've got the pile of bodies to prove it.

"Are you okay?" she asks, standing on the other side of my desk.

I stand, because I can't sit here under her dead stare for one moment longer. If I don't get this rage out of my somehow, I'm going to pull out my piece and start tearing a bunch of brand-new, shiny red holes in her skin, and that'd be far too merciful a punishment for the things she's done to me and mine.

"You can walk," she says, her surprise genuine, a flicker of fear in her cocky fucking expression. "I can't believe it. After what happened?"

She's got that smirk on her glossy lips. *How did I not realize she's got her father's mouth*? The past slams into me like a goddamn freight train as I recall that same expression on John's face, right before I put a bullet in him. He didn't know I knew he was fucking my woman. I made him understand that you do not fuck with me and get away with it. Nobody gets away with it. Not John, six and some change years ago, and not his devil fucking spawn, standing before me like a smarmy seductress, six and some change years later.

"Come here, you fucking cunt," I grind out painfully as her eyes light up. She doesn't look scared. She looks amused, standing in my office with her tiny shirt showing off her cleavage, looking just like she did when she first waltzed into my office and began her carefully planned destruction of my universe. It's time to repay the favor. I'm going to wreak vengeance upon her for taking what's mine. Four of my sons are dead.

Dead.

I can't even confront the reality of that statement. I'm practically fucking vibrating with rage, and this little slut can't see that I'm about to attack. She's got a set of brass balls, I'll give her that. Sickeningly, she reminds me of myself. She strolled into this joint like *she* owned it. Well, not anymore.

My cock hardens when I think about all the horrible things I'm going to do to her as soon as I knock her the fuck out and get her out of here.

"Whoa. You kiss your mother with that mouth?" she asks, her voice light and unencumbered by the weight of the world. My heart seizes in my chest. For a split second, I see a little girl standing on Santa Monica Pier, her hand in mine, as we line up to ride the Ferris wheel.

She's probably only four years old and her hand is sticky with ice cream, but I don't pull my grip away; I hold her hand tighter. There are crazy people in the world. I won't let her out of my sight. She's not my daughter, she's John's, but to me there's no difference. She's my responsibility. She's the daughter I never had. As long as I live, I'll always protect her.

I blink. The laptop screen plays a video on an endless loop as I watch the damning footage of *the daughter I never had*, dressed in a nightgown and bare feet, unscrew the lid to the fuel tank on my motorcycle and drop two homemade bombs inside. After she's finished with that one, she moves on to the next bike. Six bombs for five bikes, and she makes sure my bike gets two, the vengeful little cunt. Either that, or she can't fuckin' count.

I'm guessing it's the former.

There's a voice inside me that screams, "*This is your fault*," but I push that down into the blackness because shit like that doesn't help. Emotions, other than rage and cold calculation, don't work for me. They only lead to weakness. I've already shown enough weakness when it comes to this bitch, and look where it's gotten me: four dead sons, a face full of angry red shrapnel scars, and a lifetime of fucking misery and regret.

On a whim, I turn the laptop around so she can see what I see. My chest does some weird kind of jump when I see the recognition light up in her eyes when she sees what the granulated pixels are presenting to her.

Do you kiss your mother with that mouth? She'd asked me.

I smile cruelly, the bitter taste of satisfaction leeching from my tongue into my mouth as I round my desk and charge at her. She goes for the door behind her, but it slams shut, because I wasn't going to let her slip through my fingers this time. I hear Viper slide the lock into place on the other side of the door, sealing her and I inside this sarcophagus of secrets together. I see the panic in her eyes, and it makes my cock throb.

Yes. It's my turn now, you silly little girl.

I wrap my large hand around her swan-like neck, so fucking tight I could snap it in half. I lean in real close, watching her eyes go wide as terror and regret bleed together underneath the blue contact lenses that are hiding her bamboo green eyes from me. Her hands come up, scrabbling at my flesh as I squeeze harder, choking her. Her nails dig into my skin so hard they draw blood, and the sight revitalizes me.

There's going to be so much more blood in our future, and

it's going to be beautiful. I'm going to carve this cunt up like a Thanksgiving turkey, piece by painful piece; like a butcher with his blade. She'll be unrecognizable to anyone but me soon enough.

I shift my grip to her face, my hand over her mouth, and feel her greasy lip-gloss on my palm. She struggles, her fists pummelling against my chest and her knee trying desperately to find my balls, but I've got her pinned with my hips. She isn't going anywhere … not now, not ever.

"I know you think this is going to be bad," I say, pleasure and rage sizzling in my veins, "but however bad you think this is going to be, it's going to be *So.Much.Worse.*"

There's a moist rag in my pocket and I can feel it starting to seep through my jeans. I can smell the chemical on it, but it's not for me to breathe in, it's for her. Sure, I could just strangle her until she passes out, but it's easier this way—*cleaner*. My bare hands are just about ready to snap her fucking neck, and then it'll be over before her damnation has even begun. I fish the damp material from my pocket and release my grip from her jaw, only long enough to replace it with the hand that's got the chloroform-soaked rag in it. Pressing it against her beautiful fucking face, she fights me with everything she's got.

I watch the light fade in her eyes as she passes out in my grip. It takes everything inside me not to throw her on the ground and kick the shit out of her, then fuck her while I beat on her until she's no longer breathing. The beast inside me is baying for her warm blood … for her soft skin.

Do it, the voice whispers. *Tie her up and fuck her to death. Fuck her and make her bleed, then slit her throat after you've unloaded inside her.*

No.

I won't.

I have to make this last.

She must suffer.

When I'm certain she's unconscious, I let her go. She slides down the door and lands awkwardly on the stained carpet, her lips slightly parted as she breathes heavily.

Fuck it. My balls are like two weights between my legs, full of hate and lust, and begging for release. I won't fuck her, not yet. I want her eyes on me and her legs tied to bedposts when I stick my dick inside her and torture her with pleasure, but mostly pain. I want her fully aware when I press my fingers against her tight little clit while making her come and cry, all at once. I want her to know all the things I do to her, and that is the only reason I don't wrench her knees apart and slam my rock-hard cock into her right now on the floor of my office.

Instead, I pull her shirt up to expose two perfect tits, her pink nipples smooth and flat. I straddle her waist, unzipping my jeans and palming my cock with one hand, squeezing it to the point of pain. This'll be the last time I jerk off in a long time because I've got myself this little whore now, and she's just become my come receptacle for the rest of her short life. She thought she could outplay me, the fucking President of the Gypsy Brothers? The Kingpin of Venice Beach? No. I snuffed out her daddy for his betrayal, and I'll do exactly the same thing to her, only much, much slower.

I start to jerk off over her big, round tits, the movement causing them to bounce ever so softly, up and down, my balls aching at the sight. I stop only to lean down and take one nipple in my mouth, sucking until it pebbles to a hard peak. I can't help but grin. This girl is as fucked up as me. Even in her unconscious state, I feel her writhe beneath me, her breath coming faster.

Dirty whore.

I don't have long, though I'd like to take my time here. But for now, I'll settle for blowing on her before I bundle her up and move her to the compound in San Diego. I pause to unzip her jeans and pull them off so she's in front of me with her long, tanned legs.

Just a little, I think. I won't fuck her. I just want a taste of what's to come later, when she's chained like a fucking dog on the floor. I already know where I'm taking her. I'm putting her underground, where there's no light and no hope.

My cock twitches impatiently. Spreading her thighs apart, I hook a finger into her lace panties and pull them to the side, dipping one finger into her moist cunt. *My* cunt. She's deep in the chloroform-induced sleep I've bestowed upon her, but her pussy still tightens when I take my thumb and apply the slightest pressure on her clit. A wry smile spreads across my face as I remove her panties and ball them up, shoving them into her mouth. She might be dead to rights, but that shit turns me on; the way she'll choke if she wakes up and tries to draw in a breath to scream.

I've already vowed to myself that I won't fuck her, but I need to be inside her. I'm about to blow just thinking about the fear in her eyes as I take my pound of flesh, over and over, for the lives of my sons. For her arrogant assumption that she could enact her revenge on me for taking her daddy. John deserved what I did to him. He took my woman, twisted her mind until she only wanted him, and he had the audacity to try and steal my fucking son from me too. Not once, but *twice*.

I force her legs to open wider, and she's wet enough, just from where I've been touching her to slide my dick inside her pussy. I stop halfway, biting on the inside of my cheek until I taste blood, the pain bringing me back to the point of control so I don't slam my cock into her, violently. I want this magnificent torture to last, for me and for her.

My cock throbs and my balls tighten painfully. I'm only halfway inside her, and I've only been there for seconds, but her pussy contracts ever-so-slightly and I have to pull out, spilling thick ropes of come all over the tits she probably paid for with the money her fucking father and that traitorous bitch, Mariana, stole from me.

Once I've finished, I stand and admire my handiwork with a smirk. Her legs are spread wide, shaved pussy in full view. My come pools between her tits and in the hollow of her collarbone, seeping into the hem of her shirt that I've pushed up around her neck. Any last trace of guilt ebbs away as I think of what she's done to me, to my sons, and to this club. She might be the girl I watched come into this world, but that girl died. This ghost, this fucking whore, who walked into my office and presented her ass to me with her palms flat on my desk and amusement in her eyes? She should have stayed the fuck away, because nobody escapes my wrath twice.

The things I'm going to do to her.

I'm going to make her death last the rest of my life.

I'm going to hurt her. I'm going to defile her. I'm going to burn her soul away until all that's left is blood, shattered bones and screams.

I'm going to keep her alive until she begs me to let her die, but even then, I won't let her leave me. I'll never let her die. I'm going to twist her diabolical fucking soul until she's completely at my mercy; knees on the ground and her mouth on my cock, sucking and begging for forgiveness all at the same time.

I'm going to kill every single person she ever cared about, rip her fucking insides out, and only then will I let her bleed to death beneath me as I fuck the last bit of light out of her dying eyes.

Elliot's point-of-view takes place three years before Seven Sons, when he leaves Juliette and returns to Los Angeles in an attempt to bring down the Gypsy Brothers himself

Elliot

"Julz!" I said forcefully. She raised her pale green eyes to mine, and something inside my chest tightened painfully. I could always tell if it was going to be a good day or a bad day by her eyes. The lighter they were—the more washed-out—, the worse it was going to be.

It didn't make sense, but it was as if on those days, every ounce of joy and happiness had been sucked right out of her, leaving only the pain and the rage.

And there was so much pain inside this broken girl. *My girl.* It hurt me sometimes just to look at her; just to sit beside her and breathe the same air. It hurt to exist within the same life as her, to know the burdens she carried inside herself, tightly wrapped, black and desolate.

And today? Today her eyes were so pale, you'd struggle to even call them green. Whenever I saw her like this, I imagined them. The Gypsy Brothers. How I'd love to go there and burn their clubhouse to the ground, and then piss on the fucking ashes. For the things they had done to my girl. They were things so horrific, … I wouldn't even know how to begin describing them.

I remembered the night I'd had found her, almost by chance.

Three years ago, I was still a cop with the LAPD, just before everything in my world fucking imploded. I'd been called into the station at the last minute. I remembered how dog-tired I was after pulling a double shift that'd only ended five hours prior. But the flu was going around, and our precinct was falling like dominoes, one after the other. Mendoza was apparently the latest to fall prey, and we'd been working together all night. I swore to pay him back the next time we were on shift together.

I'd been mainlining cheap station coffee when the call came in over the radio from St. Andrew's hospital downtown. Normally my squad operated from our own station, Pacific Division 14, but our building was being renovated, so we were all crammed into the older LAPD building on South Spring Street.

I'd literally just turned up at the station to cover Mendoza's shift when my Captain started barking at me. My eyes felt like they were full of sand and the coffee tasted like shit. I wanted to tell the woman to back off—yes, my Captain was a five-foot-nothing African-American woman, with enough attitude to render me speechless every time she spoke. I stood still, trying to look respectful as I choked down a mouthful of the caffeinated sludge I'd just unwittingly poured into my mouth.

"Walk," Iverson barked, taking my coffee cup and tossing it in the trash. "I'll fill you in while you change." Not one to argue, I started for the locker room with a strange sense of dread starting in the pit

of my stomach. Something told me that what I was about to hear wasn't good. "Marina Del Rey," Iverson said, still following me to the men's locker room. "Go with Kennedy. He's waiting for you in the basement."

I raised my eyebrows as I took a fresh shirt from my locker and shrugged it on, buttoning it as Iverson relayed more information. She didn't seem to care that she was standing in the midst of shift change in an LAPD locker room, surrounded by dudes in various stages of undress, but regardless, I listened intently as Iverson listed more details, noting the fact that I was yet to utter a single word in this conversation.

"It's a priority case," she was saying, and I nodded as I got to fixing my belt. The last thing I did was take my Glock from the locker in front of me and snap it into the holster at my hip.

I made my way towards the basement, ready to start whatever it was Captain Iverson was skirting around. She continued to follow me, which was odd. Really, really odd. When we were halfway down, she stopped suddenly. I was a few strides ahead of her and backed up. "Everything alright, Captain?" I asked, my mouth still burning from the shitty coffee I'd forced down. I'd never seen the woman look so jumpy.

"McRae," she said, then trailed off suddenly. Something wasn't adding up.

"Is this a personal case, Ma'am?" I asked slowly.

I saw her tense. "Not really, no. But there's a girl… she's with the Gypsy Brothers." My stomach dropped when I heard that. Shit. I'd been at the scene of a murder just last month that had been the work of one of their members, and nobody would talk. The suspect, Jimmy Alvarez, had been let go on lack of evidence. Everyone knew he had shot the stripper in the back of the head, but damned if we could pin it on him. Motherfuckers were good at finding their way around the law. "She's the president's daughter," Iverson added. "She's fifteen, and she's probably going to die. She's at Marina Del Rey."

I nodded, suddenly more awake. The thought of those ruthless bikers, and what they could possibly have to do with a fifteen-year-old girl being in the hospital, had my stomach in knots. I'd seen my fair share of shit on the job, but when women got hurt, it burned me to the fucking core. I had a deep respect for females. Maybe because my grandmother had raised me almost single-handedly, and the only male role models I had were douchebags, but I sincerely believed that women were smarter, stronger, and more capable than the majority of dudes. I think Iverson recognized this in me, and she seemed to trust me with sticky situations like this. "Rival gang?" I asked, digging for something more concrete to go on. What am I walking into here?

Iverson's mouth twisted into a grimace. "Inside job," she murmured. "Don't ask me how I know ... but I know. Do whatever you have to. Do not let that girl out of your sight, you hear me?"

"Yes, Captain." Inside job? Great ... just fucking great.

Sure enough, Kennedy was waiting downstairs for me. We'd been partners before I was transferred out of central booking and put onto traffic section, before finally moving into tactical response, which is where he'd always wanted to be. Kennedy was a chubby fucker and had failed the tactical physical test. He was only twenty-nine, but he was already in danger of being pushed into a desk job if he didn't lay off the donuts.

When we arrived at the hospital, Kennedy was tasked with interviewing the bikers while I covered the girl. "Don't let her out of your sight," Iverson had said, and I wasn't going to. I strode right to her hospital room, despite the doctor telling me she was too weak to interview. I walked straight past the VP of the Gypsy Brothers, Dornan Ross, to get to her, just as he was coming out of her room. Dornan made a point of shoulder checking me as he walked past. The guy was built, about the same height as me, and wearing a leather vest with a patch sewn on that screamed, "GYPSY BROTHERS."

"You should watch where you're going," I said, my demeanor deathly calm, despite the horror that lurked beneath the surface. I wasn't afraid of this guy, but I was afraid of laying eyes on this girl and seeing what had happened to her.

"Do you know who I am?" he asked, looking me up and down, making sure I noticed the way his gaze lingered on my name badge.

I smirked, looking him up and down in response. "You got blood on your boots," I said, pointing to the spatter on the biker's steel-capped black boots. "You should get that cleaned up."

"You're observant," he replied.

I smiled a smile that contained no joy within it; only scathing. "That her blood?" I asked casually, tilting my head towards the girl in the bed who had lost so much blood, that it had to be replaced not once, but twice.

The biker looked down at his boot-clad foot, as if he were trying to decide whether he should kick me in the balls or not, but instead he grinned, baring his teeth like a fucking dog about to attack. "Well, I brought her in, so it makes sense, doesn't it?"

"Officer Kennedy will be out to talk to you," I said, dropping the smile. "Until then, I suggest you don't come back in here."

Dornan narrowed his eyes, but his "fuck you" smile remained. "I can't get a thing out of her," he said, his voice chillingly devoid of emotion. "She's too traumatized to speak. Perhaps you should come back tomorrow, boy."

I fought not to erupt. I knew I couldn't afford to show emotion; to express the rage inside my chest at people like this motherfucker who thought they were above the law. I stared at Dornan Ross and had no doubt that he had something to do with the girl's brutal attack. "She might not last that long," I replied. "Don't you want to catch the people who did this?"

Dornan puffed his chest out and stepped closer, getting up in my fucking space. I wanted to step back, but I stood my ground. "She's like a daughter to me," he said, stepping even closer, crowding me. "I think you should remember that, son."

"I'm not your son. I'm Officer McRae, Mr. Ross."

The biker smiled. "So you do know who I am."

I didn't even bother replying. I walked into the girl's hospital room and slammed the door behind me with force, letting the biker know that he was no longer welcome anywhere near this girl who was "like a daughter" to him.

The girl: the reason I was here in the first place.

I wanted to choke when I turned and saw what she'd been reduced to. I could tell she was a pretty girl, even under the layers of bruising and dried blood. Her blonde hair was knotted and unkempt; Dark bruises encircled her wrists, telling their own story. I slowly approached, afraid that even moving the air around her too fast would make her shatter and break.

Someone had carelessly tossed a bunch of flowers on the bed beside her. The girl might not be dead, but she looked like it. Only the steady beep of the heart monitor and the slight movement of her chest told me that she was still in this world. She was a mess, . Every visible part of her was bruised, or cut open, or burned. This poor girl looked broken beyond repair.

I didn't know why Iverson had even bothered sending me down. The girl was clearly not going to make it. At least, that was my attitude until she opened her eyes and sat bolt upright in bed, making me jump.

"Jesus Christ!" I yell-whispered.

"My name's not Jesus," she replied, in a husky voice that rose barely above a whisper. She coughed and coughed. I stood there, mute, before I snapped to my senses and rushed for the glass of water beside her bed. I handed it to her and she took it gratefully, sipping it between coughing fits.

"I'm Elliot," I said, pointing at myself. Fuck the formal "Officer

McRae" bullshit. She was scared and was damn near close to death. I'd spoken to the doctor briefly on the way in. She had severe internal bleeding that they couldn't stop, and swelling on the brain. She might have been able to talk, but it probably wouldn't be long before she passed out again.

"I'm Juliette," she said.

"Who did this to you?" I asked quietly. The girl, Juliette, didn't reply for a long time. She stared off into space at something I couldn't see. I didn't think she was going to answer me at all until she spoke.

"I'd rather stay alive," she'd whispered, shaking her head.

That had been three years ago, and now, that fifteen-year-old girl was eighteen, and she was in my bed. She was my girl, and I was the only thing she had in the world. Every other person who had ever loved or known her, thought she was dead. We were in love, or some fucked up version of love that I didn't fully understand.

Oh, and she had a gun in her hands.

"*Julz*," I repeated, more urgently this time. "Whatcha doin'?" My words were casual, but my tone was not. I stood at the end of my bed, our bed, and stared down at my girlfriend as she clutched my Saturday Night Special in her hands.

"Nothing," she said quietly. "Just thinking."

"Can I have that?" I gestured to the gun.

"You don't have to worry about me," she said petulantly, handing me the gun.

My heart still hammered in my chest as I took it and tucked it into the back of my jeans. "Oh, really," I replied, attempting to sound more upbeat, but failing. "I don't have to worry?"

"I wouldn't blow my brains out. It would ruin my looks. I mean, how would you have an open casket if I shot myself in the face?"

Don't talk like that, don't talk like that, DON'T FUCKING TALK LIKE THAT.

She joked like it was absurd for me to be afraid of her killing herself, and yet she'd tried to do just that …not *once*, not *twice*, but *three fucking times*. Her wrist still bore the scar from the last attempt, when I'd found her in the bathtub, full of red-tinged water. My garage still reeked of exhaust fumes after she'd left my truck running and tried to gas herself. And just last week, she'd tried to hang herself over a rafter in my storage shed. It was exhausting, trying to keep someone in this world when they didn't want to be in it. Hell, the entire world believed she was already dead, and she was trying to make it truth.

She must have seen the terror on my face because something in her expression changed. She closed off; became more resigned. It was a coping mechanism she employed regularly to stop me from getting in so she could keep her sadness from leaking out and infecting me. It didn't work, though. Her despair became mine as I watched her wither and fade away for three whole years. In rare moments, and I mean very rare, I saw her smile. I saw those green eyes turn bright as she recalled happier times, but it never lasted.

The despair always returned.

"I don't want to be your burden," she whispered, turning her sad eyes towards the floor.

"You're not," I said, sitting beside her, wrapping my arms around her fragile body. I'd burn the world down if it would make her feel one ounce of peace, but I knew she'd be just as sad and broken, no matter what I did. "I promise you're not a burden to me."

But the words that came out of my mouth were lies.

Time was supposed to heal all wounds.

But it didn't heal Juliette's.

Time gave her *too much time*; Time to relive the horrors that those sick, twisted fucks had subjected her to. She lived through them every single day without a moment's peace. And monsters was a poor word. I couldn't think of a word that adequately conveyed just how heinous they were. Beasts? Yeah. Maybe beasts was more accurate. Beasts that had ripped her apart, and destroyed her, through no fault of her own. And these boys had been her family growing up. The ringleader, Dornan Ross, had been her father's best friend. It sounded as though he'd been like a father to her, from the way she told the story.

I watched her thrashing in bed, the rope marks still clearly visible on her neck. My stomach knotted; I knew what would come next. Her mouth opened, sucking in air as her eyes opened, blank and unseeing. They were night terrors. I'd seen her have them enough times that they no longer shocked me. They just filled my gut with icy dread, and heartbreak for her, every single night.

Because of her memories and her constant suffering, I was depressed all the time, as well. I was stuck with her, and I didn't want to be. I resented her. I loved her to fucking death,, but most of all, I just wanted her to get better. However, I'd finally come to the realization that she was never going to get better.

"Hey," I said, my voice almost monotone. The way she screamed out in the night still scared the ever living fuck out of me, but at least now I knew what to expect. She'd claw at the air above her, and I'd stay out of her way. She'd thrash and battle with imaginary attackers, and I'd stay out of her way. She'd call for *him*, and a little piece of me would die inside.

"Jase!" She'd scream. She did this every night for three years until one night, I broke.

I'd started packing before the sun even rose. I tried to be quiet at first, but I decided fuck it. I'd held her three times—no, wait, four in total—while I freaked the fuck out, not knowing if she'd live through the night or not. She'd put me through hell, and didn't even care that she was hurting me, even though she knew what she was doing to me. I made a little more noise as I threw more shit in the bag.

I'd stormed towards the Mustang with nothing but a black duffel bag, crammed with clothes and very few possessions. I was leaving the only girl I'd ever loved, and I wasn't coming back.

It wasn't the fact that she'd tried to kill herself three times already. Fuck, that shit was so goddamn hard on me, but I could hardly blame her. It was a wonder she had survived at all, but was living even worth it if she lived this way for the rest of her life? I couldn't bear living my life with her this way anymore. It wasn't because she didn't love me, because she did. I knew she did. In the night, before we fell asleep, she would search for my hand in the dark, clutching it until she fell asleep. No, it was because after three years, she still called out for that bastard Ross who watched as his father and brothers destroyed a defenceless fifteen-year-old girl he claimed to love.

Jason fucking Ross.

My hatred was singularly focused on that son-of-a-bitch. I'd become obsessed with him—with all the Gypsy Brothers, but it would always come back to Jason, because he was one of *them*, and he was the one she still called out for.

Julz was awake by the time I started the Mustang and revved the engine, loud enough to wake the entire street. I was out of fucks to give. Let them complain about the noise. I wouldn't be back to listen to them anyway.

As I was debating whether to go back inside and grab my hunting rifle from the toolshed, Julz appeared in the window. One look at her face and I knew *she knew*. Her eyes were glassy, but she threw me a half-hearted smile as she tapped on the glass. Reluctantly, I rolled my window down, my dark sunglasses shielding the tears in my own eyes. I mean, I wasn't a fucking pussy, but I was pissed. Why'd we have to meet the way we did, in a goddamn nightmare? She was so beautiful and passionate in the moments her demons weren't dragging her beneath the murky waters and drowning her. Selfishly, I wished she would try harder to be that girl who laughed and said funny things, dazzling me with her smile, instead of the girl who held my gun in her lap and willed herself not to eat it.

"Going somewhere?" she asked, looking at the black duffel in the backseat.

I nodded, tearing my gaze from her.

"Yeah."

Out of the corner of my eye, I saw her trying not to cry. "Are you coming back?" I gripped the steering wheel so tight, my fingers turned white. I couldn't look at her. I couldn't even answer her. If I'd let myself get sucked into her doe-eyes again, I'd never be able to leave. I was afraid that if I stayed, I might end up killing us both to stop feeling so fucking miserable. "It's okay, Elliot," she said, trailing her hand over my cheek. "I'd leave me too, if I could." I swallowed back all the words I'd never be able to say to her. Her fingers left my face and she stepped back from the car.

I could have stayed, but I didn't. I was done. Maybe without me, she'd get better instead of sliding into the blackness until it consumed her and she really did die.

I revved the engine one last time and took my foot off the brake pedal, slamming the accelerator as hard as I could and sped away from the scene of my ruin.

Jase

The first time I saw Juliette Portland, after six years of death, I didn't even notice her. She was just a generic girl with fake tits and a dazed expression on her face as she looked around the bar, taking the place in. I barely glanced at her as I moved racks of clean beer glasses into the refrigerator, getting the bar of my father's strip club ready for another night of customers. They'd swill beer and get their rocks off as they tucked crumpled dollar bills into tiny thongs that left nothing to the imagination, and I'd fix drinks and count down the hours until I could leave.

She was wearing ridiculously short cut-offs that showed the underside of her pert ass cheeks, but she didn't even make my cock react. She looked like every other girl who walked into that strip club with stars in their eyes and left with my father's jizz on their tongues.

But looking back on that day, knowing what I know now, I think that's the hardest thing of all for me to accept inside myself. That I had the girl I thought I'd lost forever, and she was standing right in front of me, and. I could have grabbed her and taken her away from the all the madness before my father ever had the chance to lay his hands on her again; *and I didn't even know it.*

My father's dead now, and we're safe – for the moment, at least – but Juliette's retribution cost more than I could have ever fathomed. She's not the same girl I knew when we were young, and I'm not the same boy I was when we met. We're all grown up, now. And what a hellish fucking upbringing it was.

The first time I ever met Juliette Portland was in a filthy little room in the Gypsy Brothers clubhouse. Only days earlier I'd existed in a different world, where my father was a figment of my imagination instead of a ruthless biker, where we were safe from people like the Gypsy Brothers. I'd arrived home to our house in Colorado to find my mom murdered and the father I'd never met, sitting at our kitchen table, eating a fucking sandwich with her blood still on his hands. Being the stupid teenager I was, instead of running, I'd tried to fight him, and I lost. I lost everything. He knocked me out with one blow and kept me drugged in the trunk of a car for two days. When I finally woke up from my drugged slumber, I'd pissed all over myself.

I turned into a fucking animal. I lunged at them, raged at them. I even tried to escape, but I was just a kid with massive amounts of drugs in my system. I moved like a clumsy drunk, crashing into walls as I took swings at Dornan, the man who'd both given me life and returned to take it away from me. I might've been clumsy and disoriented, but I refused to let anyone within ten feet of me ... until Julz.

She crept into the room like she wasn't supposed to be there while I crouched in the corner. She was so young, so beautiful, like a fucking angel that had been sent to save me. She didn't save me, but she did bring healing ointment for the *GYPSY BROTHERS* tattoo that now took up my entire back. It had taken hours upon hours of a needle being dragged through my skin, and I'd finally passed out from the exhaustion and the drugs as my *brothers* held me down and laughed.

Funny how we both ended up waiting for the other to miraculously materialize and save the other. After they killed her, my father took me to my grandfather's compound in San Diego.

I'd had barely a year of freedom between my mother's death and Juliette's, but in that time, I'd fallen hard for John's daughter. I'd realized that he was the man who visited my mother and checked in on us, but I never uttered a word. I knew if I did, my father would probably kill him, too.

I mean, he killed him anyway, but that's not the point.

See, my father eventually found out what John had done – ; stolen his girlfriend for himself, and plotted to leave Los Angeles with Juliette and me in tow.

You don't try to take a son from Dornan Ross and survive.

My father delivered the first bullet to John himself, before he forced me to finish him off. After that, I'd spent the next three years of my life underground in a tiny cell, chained to a wall and forced to watch the video, on an endless loop, of my father and brothers raping, torturing, and beating the only girl I'd ever loved as a club whore knelt between my legs and sucked my cock.

For the first month of this, I didn't even get an erection; the horror was still so fresh. Whatever slutty girl they'd send in would spend hours sucking away at me like a leech, and I'd stare at the TV screen in front of me, willing myself to die.

By the end of the first month, I was getting hard. After three months, I was coming in whatever mouth was sucking me as I stared blankly at the horrors unfolding in front of me in black and white.

After six months, I wasn't chained anymore. I was still locked in my cell, but shit was different. The things I did to those girls. I don't even want to think about how much I enjoyed their cries of pain as I shoved them face-down into the concrete fucking floor, making them bleed from busted lips and smashed noses. Some would leave, bloody and scratched from the force of my hand shoving their faces into the hard floor. I would sink my teeth into their flesh while I fucked them as hard and as rough as I could. I no longer cared about whether they hurt or not. At least they got to leave afterwards, with their torn panties in their hands and their lipstick still on my cock. Fucking the girls my father gifted me in my chamber of horrors was the only thing I had to look forward to in my solitary existence, and watching that torturous video became so routine, I almost looked forward to the release it would bring while I sank my dick inside them.

I know. I was a sick fuck, and I still am, but I'll never tell Juliette what happened down there. I'll fucking die before I utter a word of those three years of hell to her.

There's something to be said about a person who's been put in hell and doesn't lose themselves.

But what if you *find* yourself there instead?

Growing up, I always knew I was different. The things in my mind weren't the same things that existed in others, and I knew this. My mom never told me anything about my father, other than to run for my goddamn life if he ever showed up. The way she said it scared the living shit out of me, and I never asked about him again.

I was about twelve when I figured out who he was. He scared me. I didn't want him to find us.

He did anyway.

My oldest brother, Chad, tasked himself with schooling me in the realities of fucking, after my father grew tired of the job. I'd become compliant, abusing each girl he sent into my cell worse than the last until he stopped sending them altogether. That made me mad. He'd gotten me addicted to them, and then took them away—my only form of release—, so I ended up like a fucking pervert, jerking off in the dark to a video that showed the rape of a dead girl I used to love.

My brother didn't want to fuck *me*, thank God—it wasn't like that—but he was a perverted bastard who wanted me to be one, too, just like him. He couldn't understand how I couldn't do to Juliette what he did to her after watching how I'd treated the whores my father sent to me. He knew I'd hurt every single girl my father sent down to my cell, but it was different. I wasn't raping anyone. Dear old Dad was paying them to come fuck me, so I had no problem making them work for their money … and then some. He was fucking with me, and I was fucking his whores right back.

So one day, my brother introduced me to a different girl; a girl who I wasn't allowed to fuck. A girl I was supposed to *respect*. I wanted to fuck her, of course. I wanted to force her to her knees and squeeze her cheeks until she opened her mouth and took my cock all the way down her throat until she gagged. I wanted to hold her against the wall and choke her while I fucked her.

I was turning into my father, and I didn't even care.

She was skinny, pale, with reddish hair that hung limply around her long face. Waifish was the word you'd use to describe her, but after weeks of no girls to take care of my needs, all I saw was an empty vessel to stick my dick in.

She actually stuck her hand out to shake mine, and I recoiled. Chad snickered.

"He doesn't get out much," he supplied helpfully. I glowered at him. The girl shrugged, apparently unperturbed by my lack of social skills.

"You can call me Rails," she said.

Chad snorted. "Because you're built like a fuckin' rail? Take some of your whorin' money and buy yourself a push-up bra, for Christ's sake. You look like you're twelve." She rolled her eyes at him and I felt a smile twitch at my lip, but I didn't dare show it. This girl was rolling her eyes at crazy Chad, and suddenly, I didn't want to just fuck her, I wanted to know her.

After that, Rails was the only girl I'd touch. I didn't fuck her—I refused to fuck her. I did just about everything else with her, though. She sucked cock like a pro. And while I didn't love her, I came to rely on her … even need her. She visited me every week. Sometimes, she'd even bring a friend, and I'd have no trouble fucking them, but I could never bring myself to have sex with Raelene.

It was almost as if she reminded me of a girl I used to love.

"Fuck me," Rails whispered. "Fuck me and they'll let you leave. It's your birthday today and it's warm outside. Don't you want to feel the sun on your face?"

I let out a whoosh of air, hot water pricking at my eyelids. I hadn't cried in years, not since Juliette. But for some reason, the tender concern in Raelene's voice made me want to scream. I'd been holding off her suggestions and advances for so long, I couldn't bear the thought of poisoning her with my sick brand of fun that made women scream.

"I can't," I whispered. "You're too good for me. I'll hurt you, Rails."

"Put your hand on my neck," she whispered. I swallowed thickly.

"I don't want to hurt you," I protested. She shook her head, a wan smile on her lips.

"You won't hurt me," she replied, straddling my hips, my cock already leaking with pre-cum as I thought about slamming her down on me until her eyes rolled back in her head and she begged me to stop. The thought caused a hot blade of shame to stab into my gut and twist painfully.

Why did I want to make her cry? What the fuck was wrong with me?

Maybe I could be softer with her. Maybe I wouldn't have to hurt her. She was the first human being I'd cared about in any way since Juliette had been ripped from my arms and brutalized by first Chad, then the rest of my fucked -up brothers, before my father swooped in and finished the job.

"Just tell me," I whispered. "How long have I been in here?"

"A little over three years," she whispered back. She rocked her hips against me and I struggled with the desire to impale her with my rock-hard erection. God, I wanted to fuck her. I wanted more release than I could get from her hands, or her mouth. I could be good to her, couldn't I? I didn't have to hurt her to satisfy myself. As it was, it'd been so long since I sank into a wet, warm pussy, I was about to come just from the friction of her cotton-covered cunt rubbing along my cock.

She'd already unbuckled my pants and had me in her hands, under the pretense of blowing me when she'd seemed to change her mind, crawling onto my lap instead. "I want you inside me."

"I can't," I protested.

"Let me do it for you," she said, lifting her hips and lining her pussy up with my cock. Just the feeling of the tip at her entrance made me want to flip her over and punish her with a good, hard fucking. I fisted the sheets and squeezed hard enough that I heard my joints pop.

"Jesus, fuck…" I groaned as her hot, slick pussy slid down my cock. She was so tight, it was bordering on painful. She let out a little gasp as I filled her completely, and started to rock against me. I pushed harder into her and she winced in pain, her pupils big and round. I was hurting her, and I had barely moved inside her. I looked down to where our bodies met and saw blood. "What the … you're a virgin?" Shame rushed through me as I saw her swollen pussy lips stretched around my dick, painted red with her blood. I'd just taken her virginity in a filthy room in a corner of my grandfather's dank drug compound.

Her cheeks reddened. "It doesn't matter," she said, her breath straining around my hands on her neck. "It's no big deal." I let my hands fall from her neck to my sides, letting my head fall back onto the pillow.

She'd tricked me. She'd presented herself as some kind of whore, and it turned out she was a fucking virgin? This had to be Chad's handiwork.

"Get off me," I said, my voice monotone.

"Jason—"

"Get. Off. Me. Now!"

I thought of Juliette. I always thought of Juliette and how she'd been a virgin until they'd defiled her. I looked up at Rails, her hair hanging like a curtain around our faces; like we were the only two people in the world. "Tell me you love me," she whimpered, guiding my hands to her clit. I stilled beneath her, confused. "You don't have to mean it," she said as she began bouncing herself up and down.

So fucking tight.

"Just say it. I need it. *Please.* Just say the words and make me come."

I closed my eyes and imagined Juliette. "I love you," I whispered, one thumb rubbing Raelene's clit and the other lifting her up and slamming her back down onto me.

"Ohhhhh," she sighed, her walls tightening as she orgasmed around my cock. I moaned, coming inside her so hard I couldn't see for a few seconds. She collapsed on my chest, our bodies slick with sweat, my dick still hard inside her and ready to go again. My need was insatiable. I could fuck until I was red raw, and even the pain of that wouldn't stop me.

My shame at unwittingly deflowering Rails overpowered my own desire to keep screwing her, however, and I willed my cock to calm down until she recovered.

We lay there for several seconds, our breath coming out in laboured gasps. As moments go, it was peaceful. Calm, even.

Then, in an instant, it all shattered.

I heard footsteps approaching, along with clapping. I pushed Rails off me and she cried out. I'd probably hurt her, flinging her off me like that, but old habits die hard, and I didn't want someone sneaking up on me while I was in the throes of post-fuck bliss.

It was Chad. Built like a fucking tank, I was already half a head taller than him. He'd inherited our father's psychosis, but then, perhaps we all had. Mine had just remained dormant until somebody had given me no other coping mechanism to survive. Chad, though, delighted in tormenting anyone weaker than him. I hated him the most, because although all of my brothers had participated in raping Juliette all those years ago, Chad had taken a perverse pleasure in stealing her virginity. Every other one of them had either covered her face, or looked at the floor. A few turned her on her stomach so they didn't have to look into the eyes of a girl they'd grown up with as they stole pieces of her soul, but not Chad. He'd stared into her eyes and kissed her on the mouth as he was the first one to rip her apart, only pulling away when she bit a chunk out of his tongue.

He was a complete fucking psychopath, and I saw a glint of something in his eyes now as he stood on the other side of the open doorway that separated me from the rest of the world. I wondered, briefly, if I could overpower him and get out. I wondered if I could kill him with my bare hands before he could draw the gun at his hip and shoot me dead. "How's your pussy, Rails?" he cooed, chewing on a toothpick he'd wedged between his teeth. "You sore, baby? Want me to kiss it better?" He pulled the toothpick from his mouth long enough to snake his tongue out suggestively at her, before biting down on the toothpick again. She didn't answer him, just pulled the threadbare sheets around her like some kind of toga.

"Get dressed, both of you," Chad said abruptly. "We're going for a little walk. Dad's orders." He waggled his eyebrows at me, winking at Rails.

I hadn't been outside in three years. "No," I said, acting bored, a dull sense of panic crawling up from my bloody cock, settling in my stomach and bubbling up in my throat like acidic bile. I was the king of this three-by-three cell, and I'd resigned myself to the fact that I wasn't ever leaving it a long time ago. Beside me, Rails had dropped the sheets and was pulling her dress over her head. I saw smears of blood on her thighs and winced.

I'd done that. I'd taken something from her, and I didn't like the feeling.

Ten minutes later, I was covering my eyes with my hands. More of my brothers had joined Chad after my initial refusal to step outside, and though I was like a beast in a cage, it was still six against one. They pinned me down and zip-tied my hands in front of me, marching me outside as Rails pleaded with them to be gentle. I didn't give a fuck about me. I gave a fuck about *her*. I liked her, and she was the only friend I had in the world.

What did that mean for her?

The sun. Holy Jesus, the sun was burning me. I felt like I might die under the power of its rays, burning into my eyes. My vision filled with solid white and I would have collapsed had it not been for my brothers dragging me through the dirt yard beside Emilio's mansion.

We stopped beside a patch planted with lemon and orange trees, the sweet smell of rotting citrus faint, but almost unbearable to someone who'd been deprived of their senses for years. The hands holding me let me go and I fell to my knees in the sand. "Three years," Chad said, looking at Rails impatiently. "It took you three years, brother, but we finally broke you."

"What?" Panic churned inside me.

"You finally did it," Chad grinned, standing behind Rails and yanking her dress down to expose her taut nipples. I cringed, but I couldn't look away. I wanted to kill him, this sadistic fuck whose mission in life was to corrupt me; to make me like him. Rails didn't move, or even look alarmed. She was swaying on her feet and I saw a thread of blood in the crook of her elbow.

"You drugged her?" I asked Chad.

Chad shrugged. "She asked for it. That's her reward for visiting you, lover boy." I swallowed thickly, looking at the ground. It didn't matter. I didn't love her, and even though I hadn't been in it for so fucking long, I understood the way the world worked. It fucking burned that she'd been visiting me for years and was being paid just like the others, but in smack. Hell, maybe that's how they all got paid.

I'd known she was a drug user, but I didn't think this was the reason for her visits. I don't know what I thought, but whatever it was, I was wrong to think she was anything more than a junkie, using me to get her next fix. Yeah, no friend of mine.

I hadn't loved her, but I'd thought she maybe loved me.

"You love her?" Chad asked, and before I could blink, he had his gun in his hand, the barrel pressed against her temple. She didn't appear concerned though, floating on a wave none of us could see.

"It's okay," Rails said, her words thick. "You know how I met your brother? I was about to jump off a bridge, but he stopped me. He told me there was somebody I had to meet." She laughed, in a daze. Her eyes couldn't even focus on me. I got to my feet and lunged towards them, but my brothers held me back.

Just like before. First Juliette, and now Raelene.

I struggled and kicked like a wounded tiger as Chad took his free hand and trailed it down from her chest to her concave stomach, hiking her dress up to reveal the bloody juncture of her thighs. "You did this, and this makes you no better than us, you understand?"

"Fuck you!" I roared, bucking against the iron grip that held me back. Six against one. How was it never a fair fight? Were they really so afraid of the fact that I might beat them one-on-one?

"Say it," Chad said, sliding one finger inside Rails so that she flinched. Even with the drugs, the rough way he was poking and prodding at her must have hurt. "Say you're no better than us. Say you're one of us and I'll let her go." I looked to Rails, but she wasn't even there. Whatever drug was in her bloodstream, it looked effective.

"I'm no better than you." I ground out.

"And?" Chad prompted, snaking his tongue out to lick Raelene's earlobe.

I shuddered.

"And I'm one of you."

"One of what?"

"A fucking Gypsy Brother!" I screamed.

Apparently satisfied, Chad took his hands off Rails, letting her sway unsteadily on her own. Before I could move, he blew her brains out. Took his gun, pressed it to the back of her head and pulled the trigger. The bullet didn't just enter her head—it blew the top of her skull clean off. She fell to the ground, dead, her tits still out and her dress hiked up enough to show everything. I stared blankly as Chad spat and took another drag of his cigarette. He threw the smoldering butt on the ground beside Rails, crushing it beside her dead face with the heel of his heavy boot.

I lost it. I fucking lost it. Her blood was still smeared on my dick, her brains arranged around her head like a perverse halo, and she wasn't going to wake up from this.

"You fucking pussy!" I roared. I pulled so hard, I broke the zip-strip that bound my wrists together and began tearing at arms and hands until I was free. I stood, balling my fists so hard I swear I felt my own bones splintering under the weight of my rage. Six against one, but none of my brothers could have stopped three years of pent-up fury as I lunged at Chad, whose smirk was quickly replaced by fear. He looked to our brothers, but perhaps they, too, were tired of Chad's psychotic behavior because none of them moved particularly fast to stop me.

I rained blows down on Chad, who might have been burly, but who was also incredibly slow compared to me. I was used to moving like a panther in the dark in my cage, and I'd already broken his jaw, his nose, and shattered his knee before I could be subdued.

"So you *did* love her," Chad said, coughing up blood. I hadn't killed him, but if I'd had more time, I would have smashed my fists into him until his face looked just like Raelene's.

I looked at Rails her one last time. There was no point in being upset. I'd mourn her alone, away from these motherfuckers.

"Love her?" I spat, pulling my arms free from Maxi and Ant,

who'd pulled me off Chad so I didn't kill him. "She was a fucking junkie. I didn't love her."

"Huh.," Chad said, cradling his broken jaw as he stared up at me accusingly, "but you'd beat me to fuckin' death because I shot *that junkie*?"

I shrugged my shoulders, swiping the pack of cigarettes from Chad's shirt pocket and lighting one up. "You just wasted pussy," I said, glaring down at my brother. "You know how tight that was?"

Chad laughed. "Tight as Julz? Guess you'll never know, huh?"

I didn't react. I knew this was my test. If I broke down now, I'd be in that cell for the rest of my life, or worse—dead beside Raelene.

"She's still warm," I said, kicking Raelene's limp foot to open her legs wider. "Maybe you should try her out before she goes stiff and let me know. No point in wasting perfectly good pussy just because she's got no pulse, right?"

Everyone fell silent. The only sounds were Chad's heavy breathing and the *dripdripdrip* of blood from his nose onto the dirt ground.

"Guess you *are* a Gypsy Brother," Chad said in disbelief, and for the first time, I believed him.

The first few months after Juliette and I found each other again, I didn't fuck her—I made love to her. I was tender. I was gentle. I loved her, but it killed me to hold back. Now I don't have to hold back.

Now, she likes it better when I hurt her.

I like that flicker of panic in her eyes as she feels my hand tighten around her neck. I wonder if she thinks about *him*.

Of course she does. He's all she thinks about.

Then there's the moment of recognition; when she remembers

it's me—the one who loves her, Jase—holding her life in my grip, and she relaxes. She trusts me.

I push into her one more time, my greed at getting off even more apparent than hers. I tighten my grip and cut off her air supply, and only then do her eyes roll back in her head as her pussy clenches tight around me and we come together.

She thinks I'm appeasing her by being violent. She doesn't know about the beast that's laid dormant in me all this time. If she did, I think she'd leave me, and I couldn't bear for that to happen. I can't lose her again … I *won't.*

Normal men don't want to hurt the women they love.

Normal men don't have this darkness inside them.

But I'm not normal. I never was. I might've been patched in by force, but it doesn't change the fact that I've got *GYPSY BROTHERS* forever etched into my skin. It doesn't change the fact that I've got Ross blood running through my veins.

I might look like a good person on the surface, but it doesn't change the fact that I'm Dornan Ross's son.

I'm not sure if that's the thing that'll keep us together, or the blow that will force us apart.

ABOUT THE AUTHOR

Lili is a *USA Today* bestselling author who has sold over a million books since January 2014. After the success of her self-published Gypsy Brothers series, she was approached by HarperCollins Publishers, who signed her CARTEL series in a three-book deal. The Gypsy Brothers series focuses on a morally bankrupt biker gang and the girl who seeks her vengeance upon them. The Cartel series is a trilogy of full-length novels that explores the beginnings of the club and the drug kingpin who attempts to control its members.

Lili is also the author of psychological thriller *Gun Shy* and the *California Blood* series.

Aside from writing, her other loves in life include her gorgeous husband and beautiful daughter, good coffee, Tarantino movies and spending hours on Instagram. She loves to read almost as much as she loves to write.

You can follow her at www.lilisaintgermain.com

Jase and Julz WILL BE BACK – but in the meantime, have you read the CARTEL series? Go back to the beginnings of the GYPSY BROTHERS MC, to the first blood Dornan Ross and John Portland drew… and meet the woman who began their descent into destruction.

Cartel

Mariana Rodriguez is the eldest daughter of a Colombian drug lord. Growing up in Villanueva, Colombia, she has never wanted for anything. Private schools, a lavish lifestyle, and the safety of the Cartel that her father works for.

At nineteen, she's got her entire life mapped out, and what a good life it's going to be: graduate from college, move to America, and finally be free from the stifling grip of the Cartel.

Only, her father messes up. A shipment of cocaine - a very large, very valuable shipment - is seized by the authorities whilst under his care and he becomes liable for the debt. Half a million dollars' worth of cocaine.

Half a million dollars he does not have.

But he has a daughter, a very smart one, a daughter who would give up her very existence and offer herself as payment for her father's sins, to ensure her family survives.

But falling in love with the man who owns her isn't part of the plan …

Kingpin (Cartel, #2)

They say love conquers all.

It's a lie.

For eight years I had been the property of the Gypsy Brothers

Motorcycle Club. I laundered their money so well they'd never let me leave. My only glimmer of light was the man I loved. The man who had saved me.

Dornan.

His love had been the only thing that kept the demons at bay. But he'd become so immersed in the cartel's brutal business that I hardly knew him anymore.

Dornan had been my salvation, but he was also my undoing.

Would he pull me down into the darkness until he destroyed me? Could I save him?

Did I even want to?

Empire (Cartel, #3)

People aren't born monsters.

They're created.

I'd been with Dornan Ross for the better part of a decade. Slept in his bed, sewn up his wounds, tasted his blood, seen inside his soul.

But even I wasn't prepared for what he did.

I should have known it would always come down to this, from the very moment I laid eyes on him in that motel.

I should have known his salvation was too good to be true.

Because it's all gone now, the impossible love I had for him bleeding away in the darkness that came afterward.

Now there's only hate.

Now I just want to escape.

Even if it means I have to kill him to be free.

FREEDOM
GYPSY
BROS

Made in the USA
Middletown, DE
09 March 2019